MAEVE'S GIRLS

CHRISTINE GAEL

INTRODUCTION

La Pierre, Louisiana had never seen anything like Maeve Blanchard, and they never will again. After 75 years, five husbands, four daughters, and one bootleg whiskey ring, Maeve has finally been called home to be with the Lord...or with someone, somewhere, at any rate.

But while Maeve took her impending demise in stride, her four girls have had their worlds turned upside down.

There's 54-year-old Lena, Maeve's love child who left home at sixteen to get away from the stain of her mother's wild life and never looked back. Kate, who married far too young and lost herself somewhere along the way. Sasha, who has followed in her mother's high-heeled footsteps and is forced to come face to face with the demons from her past. And Maggie, Maeve's niece who she raised as her own.

Despite the complex relationships they shared with their mother in life, Maeve's girls each need to make their peace with her in death, and they're finally ready to come home to La Pierre to do it. The only question now is whether La Pierre is ready for them...

MAEVE

If you're reading this, that means I've gone to the big casino in the sky. And frankly, I'm not sorry. Especially if it's hurricane season.

I know some of y'all aren't going to be happy about being back in La Pierre (especially you, Lena, bless your heart). But I have faith in your ability to survive most anything, for a time. It's a trait you girls share with your mama...and cockroaches, ha! But it's also a trait that has served me very well. And, now that you've each had a chance to get a little more living under your belts, I hope you'll realize that it's served you well, too.

What comes next will probably seem like a punishment to at least two out of the four of you, but time is short, and I can't be fussed to write out the whole thought process behind my decision with the little I have left. For now, I hope you'll trust that this wasn't some random scheme I cooked up just to get on your nerves one last time.

For starters, as you know by now, I've advised Alistair that y'all need to come home for the reading of this will. There will be no

1

disbursement of funds or property until or unless that happens. I've already told him that calling in on some newfangled video program like MyFace, or some intercom doo-hickey, doesn't count. I want all four of you, same room, no exceptions (unless one of you has beaten me to the grave after the writing of this letter, something I pray to any god that has a mind to hear me won't be the case). If you're listening to this, though, that means you've all done what you were told for once, and I've already achieved in death what I couldn't in life. Somebody get the holy water, it's a miracle! But that also means each of you is struggling right now. Whether it's because I'm gone, or because you're here in La Pierre, try to be kind and patient with each other. It's going to be a long three months.

'Why?' you ask?

Because that's how long the four of you will need to live in Blanchard Manor before the deed and ownership of everything inside it will be transferred into your names. What you do with it after that is none of my concern. Sell it. Raze it. Make it into a hippy commune or a taco stand. I don't care. Beyond that, I ask of you the following:

Check on Harold for me. He's not the same since Annalise passed and he needs looking after.

Be careful with the jewelry. Lord knows, I love it gaudy, but some of it looks fake even though it isn't. Whatever you do, though, don't get it appraised down at Elsie's Gems and Antiquities. (Sorry, Alistair, I know she's your sister-in-law, but we both know she'd rob a blind man of his cane if she had the chance. Plus, she's never gotten over me winning that blue ribbon with the pecan pie I picked up at the Piggly Wiggly back in seventy-nine.)

And, last but not least, when clearing out the house, start from the attic and work your way down. That seems to be the order of things, doesn't it? The dusty old memories at the top, down to the stuff we use every day in our living spaces. But I'm also hoping that you'll come to view me a little less harshly if you start at the beginning. If you still feel the same way about me in three months as you do now? Well, that's all right, too. At the end of the day, closure is what I'm looking for here. Both for you girls and for me, too. Even if that means some of y'all closing the door and never looking back again.

Most of all, know this...

I did the best I could with what I had at the time, and gave you all the love I had to spare.

XOXO

-Maeve

LENA

Alistair Raynaud, Attorney at Law, slipped off his glasses and cleared his throat as he laid the swath of papers on his desk. "I'm afraid that's all, for right now."

Lena wasn't surprised to see the sheen of tears in his tired eyes. Alistair and her mother had known each other for nearly seven decades, and he'd been on retainer since the Nixon era. He'd handled all of the details of Maeve's annulment, both late in life divorces, and the untimely death of two spouses, making sure her interests were always looked after. He'd also kept her out of the slammer more times than any of them could count.

By Lena's estimation, Alistair was probably weeping for the loss of his best client as much as he was at having to say goodbye to a friend.

From her vantage point directly behind her sisters, Lena could see Sasha's tanned, bare shoulders shaking, and Kate as she dabbed at her own cheeks with a handkerchief, while Maggie's soft sobs filled the otherwise silent room.

But Lena's eyes were dry as a bone.

Maeve was dead right when she'd assumed that her eldest daughter would rather chew off her own leg than be back in the bear trap that was her hometown of La Pierre, Louisiana. In fact, Lena would've given up her entire inheritance to be anywhere else right now...

On that note, she stood and slid the strap of her purse over her shoulder, her legs surprisingly shaky.

"Look, I know my sisters are going through a tough time, and I don't want to add to that, so I'm going to make this quick and to the point. I don't want it," she said firmly. "I don't want any of it," Lena repeated for good measure, shooting a stiff smile at Alistair. "If you can just write up a release of some kind that I can sign in order to hand my share over to my sisters, I'll be on my way. I'm happy to pay you for your time."

She spared a quick glance at her watch and winced. Her flight back to Seattle didn't leave for another ten hours, which meant she had a good seven to spare. She made a mental note to check the movie times at the cinema near the airport. A double feature with a large popcorn there, followed by a double scotch and soda at the airport, and just maybe she'd get rid of the bad taste in her mouth.

She looked up to find Sasha staring at her over her shoulder, wide cornflower eyes full of resentment. "Are you serious right now? Mama is dead, and you're going to breeze in and breeze out in less than twenty-four hours like it's nothing?"

Lena resisted the urge to turn on her sensible heels and walk. This was one of the seven hundred reasons she hadn't wanted to come back here. The drama. Everything Maeve-related fairly oozed with it. Get too close, it'd rub off on a body and cling, like the sticky underside of a garden snail on a cobblestone pathway.

Worse, though? Once it was on you, there was no way to ever truly get it off. Nobody knew that better than Lena.

She took a steadying breath and met Sasha's accusing gaze, once again momentarily taken aback by how much she favored Maeve. Ten years younger than Lena, at 44, Sasha could've easily passed for 39 and, if Lena were to guess, probably did whenever possible. Her face was heart-shaped, like their mother's, only slightly more round, which gave her an air of innocence. Her almost preternaturally blue eyes tilted up at the corners just a little, and glinted with mischief, as if to say, *"Dare me"*. The contrasting effect was lethal. Men desired her almost as much as other women despised her.

Dolly may have pled for the mercy of an intoxicating temptress named Jolene, but she might as well have been singing to Sasha. That apple had fallen directly in front of the tree that was Maeve. Maybe that was why Lena couldn't hold her sister's gaze for very long without looking away...

She shoved those thoughts aside and tried to keep her tone even and calm as she tried again. "Having me here is only going to make things worse for you three," she reasoned. "I'm not good at pretending. Never have been. You all know it," she added, sparing a glance at her other two sisters, who had turned and now looked on in silence. "Why do that to yourselves?"

Or me.

"Ah, actually," Alistair said, his voice cutting through the tension vibrating like a live wire between them, "I'm afraid that isn't really an option anyway, Lena."

Her pulse skittered as she turned her attention to the old man behind the desk.

"What does that mean?" she demanded in a low voice.

Alistair shifted his considerable girth in the chair, making it squeal in protest, before reaching for a second, unopened envelope on his desk.

He held it up with a wry smile. "For what it's worth, I advised her against this, girls..."

Lena instantly bristled at the way he addressed them—even her youngest sister was over forty, for crying out loud—but her irritation fizzled away as she read the words scrawled across the front of the envelope in her mother's no-nonsense handwriting.

Part deux, to read when Lena tries to walk out...

Ah, Maeve, you wily old so and so. Lena let out a breath, shoulders going ramrod straight. Amazing that her mother was no longer of this earth and still found a way to get under her skin so completely.

She inclined her head but refused to retake her seat. "Get on with it, then."

Alistair tore open the envelope and perched his glasses on the end of his nose before beginning to read.

Should any of my children leave town before the three months is up, or forfeit their share, my entire estate will go to the La Pierre

*Improvement and Beautification Committee, in honor of the city
I loved so dearly. The estate will be split four ways, or not at all.*

Meaning, if she left before the three months was up, not only
would her sisters be left with nothing, but the town that had
been an albatross around her neck since the day she was born
would get a three-quarter of a million dollar makeover. Because,
apparently, Maeve had decided that a right hook was always
better when followed by a bone-jarring uppercut.

Lena pinched her eyes closed and shook her head slowly, a low
laugh escaping her lips.

Well played, Mother.

Diabolical? Yup. Manipulative? Definitely. Risky? Always. But
in life, as in death, Maeve Blanchard had never been stupid.
She'd known exactly what she was doing.

Lena didn't wait to hear more as she forced her feet into motion.

"Where are you going?" Sasha demanded, her voice shrill.

"Lena, at least listen to what else Alistair has to say," Maggie
added.

But it was Kate's words that stayed with her long after the door
closed behind her.

"Leave her be. She won't go far. She just needs some time to get
her head straight."

~

"Double scotch and soda with a twist, please."

8

Lena settled onto the barstool with a groan and kept her eyes cast down as the bartender shuffled off to make her drink. It had been years since she'd shown her face in La Pierre. Prior to that short visit, it had been almost a decade. Surely no one would recognize her. She looked nothing like the brash young woman who'd left town at age sixteen as if the hounds of hell were nipping at her heels. She'd made damn sure of it.

"You're one of Maeve's girls, aren't you?"

Less than two minutes, and the jig was already up. Swallowing a sigh, she turned to find a man in his late sixties seated at the short section of the L-shaped bar, eying her with something akin to pity. The only question was, did he feel sorry for her because her mother had died, or because Maeve had been her mother at all? Both would check out.

"I am, yes," she acknowledged with a nod. "Lena."

He squinted, scratching at one bushy eyebrow with a greasy fingernail as he studied her. "One of Vinnie's daughters?"

"Nope. That would be my sisters, Kate and Sasha."

The bartender returned with Lena's drink and set it on the bar before hitching a hip against a cooler filled with frosty beer mugs.

"Claire's daughter, then? That was a dang shame, her passing so young. Car accident, yeah?"

"Actually, that's my sister, Maggie. Maeve adopted her when my Aunt Claire died in the wreck."

This was what happened when your family tree was more like a tawdry tangle of gnarled branches than it was a mighty oak or a proud sequoia. People asked questions...made judgments. Didn't matter that she was now a fifty-four-year-old tenured professor at one of the finest universities on the West Coast, with two doctorates under her belt. When she came back to La Pierre, at one point or another, she reverted back to that shame-filled little girl without a daddy.

"So you're Clyde's, then?" he asked, frowning.

"No," she snapped coldly, not qualifying her answer this time.

"Criminy, Pete, get off the woman's back already," the bartender said, rifling through her apron pockets. "I'm sure she's had a hard day already and doesn't need you grilling her like a T-bone right now. Here," she said, handing him a wrinkled dollar bill. "Go put something happy on the jukebox, would you?"

Lena met the other woman's gaze and mouthed a furtive *"thank you"*. She hadn't taken the time to notice before, but the woman looked faintly familiar.

"Ruthie Fontaine," the bartender supplied with a smile. "We were in high school together before you..." She trailed off, picked up a white rag, and began to wipe down the well-worn bar top.

Ruthie Fontaine.

Lena cast her memory back and tugged out the cobweb-covered image of a young girl with golden hair, bright eyes and a quick smile, just a year ahead of Lena.

"I remember, now. You were valedictorian," she recalled out loud before she could stop herself. She was usually pretty good in social situations, but reminding Ruthie of that fact while she was in the middle of a Tuesday shift at a crummy bar in the same dead end town they'd both grown up in had surely been a misstep.

Ruthie's golden hair had faded to the color of dishwater, but her smile was as quick and easy as Lena remembered.

"Yeah, I was kind of a big deal back then. That and a buck will buy me a coke," she shot back, tossing the rag into the sink beside her. "Seriously, though, I had considered trying to work for NASA but then decided it would be way better for myself and future generations of Fontaines if I got knocked up my first semester at college, came home with my tail between my legs, and lived in my parents' garage for ten years. Lucky thing, too, because otherwise I wouldn't have all this." She raised both hands to gesture around the bar, her wry grin still firmly in place and holding barely a trace of bitterness. "I've used my big old brain and done the math. By my calculations, I should be able to retire by the time I'm ninety-six, so...living the dream."

Lena was surprised to find that the tension after her awkward gaffe was gone and she was smiling back at Ruthie, her mood lifting a little. "Well, I think you made an excellent decision. It's not like you can get endless, bottom-shelf gin and free pickled eggs at Yale, am I right?"

Ruthie let out a guffaw that was so genuine, it made Lena chuckle in response. This was good. Exactly what she'd needed. A few minutes to shut her brain off and not think about Maeve's death or the sticky mess that awaited her back at Blanchard Manor.

Lena was about to ask Ruthie if she was allowed to have a drink on the job when the strains of a familiar tune poured from the jukebox, forcing a groan from the other woman.

"Seriously, Pete?" Ruthie shouted across the room. "I said a happy song, for crying out loud."

It was only when the violin kicked in that Lena recognized the melody.

Dust in the Wind.

Perfect.

KATE

Blanchard Manor looked much the same as she remembered it, although she hadn't seen it in a few years. The once-cheery yellow paint showed signs of wear, the wraparound porch sagged a little, and the grounds had lost some of their former grandeur. Then again, the same could be said for Kate herself, so she wasn't about to judge. Instead, she'd receive the gift in the spirit it was given and be grateful for it. Lord knew they could use the money the place would bring once they'd sold it. She made a decent living as a school nurse, but with summers off, Frank's hours being cut at the warehouse, and their house in Shreveport mortgaged to the hilt, they were running on fumes.

"You honestly think she's going to stick around?" Sasha asked, blowing a wisp of blond hair from her eyes as she stared out at the horizon.

The heat was July thick, and Kate took a long pull from her sweaty glass of sweet tea before she answered her younger sister. "Yup."

"You're always giving her the benefit of the doubt and I have no idea why," Sasha said, crossing her legs in the hammock as she took a careful sip from her whiskey sour, leaving a smear of crimson on the goblet where her lips had been. "Her highness thinks her crap don't stink and doesn't say boo to any of us except on Christmas, when she lowers her standards to call. Still, you think she walks on water. I'll never understand why," she added with an indignant sniff.

"I'm surprised she came, myself," Maggie said from her perch on the rocking chair in the corner. "Don't get me wrong, I love Lena...always have. I just thought she'd avoid coming back if she could help it."

Maggie was right. If Lena could've helped it, she likely wouldn't have come back. But as much as she'd tried to cut this town off like a festering limb—along with everyone in it—family was family. When push came to shove and it mattered most, their big sister would come through for them. She always did, whether the others realized it or not.

"She'll be here," Kate said quietly, as sure of that as she'd ever been about anything.

A low drone filled the air around them, joining the cacophony of bullfrogs croaking and crickets chirping. The mosquitoes had apparently gotten the memo that the sun was going down, and came to feast as if on a timer, sending Kate to her feet.

"Well, she's only got until midnight to get her ass here, or we're all kissing our inheritance goodbye," Sasha said, swinging her bare feet off the hammock and standing to join Kate. "I don't know about y'all, but I'm not about to let them sell everything our mama worked for and give it to those old biddies on that beautification committee because of some ancient feud between her and Lena. I'm giving her another hour, then I'm going out to find her."

Assuming she was still in La Pierre, that wouldn't be hard to do. Lena had cut ties with any friends she'd had before skipping town at the age of sixteen, and hadn't made any attempts to reconnect with them during the handful of times she'd visited over the years. Plus, there was only one place open after eight PM. Crawdad's Pub. Sasha would cause a scene if she went there and found Lena, so Kate sincerely hoped that her oldest sister was near done moping.

As the three of them filed into the house to escape the swarm of bloodsuckers, Maggie veered off upstairs to change. Kate was just contemplating whether or not to text Lena when she heard a car door slam.

"That's probably her now," Kate said, heading back toward the door to peek out.

"Or one of the three remaining souls in a twenty-mile radius who hasn't dropped off a pie or a casserole yet," Sasha said, a hand on one lean hip as she waited for confirmation from Kate.

Thinking she might be right, Kate pressed her face against the dusty window to see Lena making her way up the path. Just short of the porch, she paused to run her fingers over the garish fuchsia blooms of the azaleas that flanked the pathway. Then, she tipped her face to the sky for a long moment, as if pleading to the heavens above. Whether she was praying for strength, guidance, or death, Kate couldn't be sure. The one thing she did know was that her big sister wasn't nearly as unaffected by Maeve's death as she pretended to be.

"Is it her?" Sasha asked, sidling up next to Kate and casting a glance out the window.

"Yeah."

Sasha turned away wordlessly, crossing the creaky pine floors to return to her seat and the box of pictures she'd been going through before they'd gone outside for a spell.

There was a firm rap on the door, followed by a long moment of silence.

"Figures she'd knock on the door of her own dang house," Sasha muttered as Kate bustled into the foyer.

She pulled the door open and wordlessly stepped to the side for Lena to come in.

"The gang's all here, I imagine?" Lena murmured.

The faint, though not unpleasant, smell of whiskey clung to her breath, but there was no indication that her older sister was drunk or anywhere near it. For that, Kate was grateful. Sasha was two whiskey sours in, herself, and adding a lot of liquor into the other side of an already tricky equation would be a recipe for more disaster.

"Yeah. Maggie is upstairs changing. We were all going through some boxes. Figured we might as well get started."

No comment from Lena on the fact that Kate wasn't the least bit surprised to see her, or that she and the others had begun the daunting task of sorting the house without being certain that the items inside were even theirs to sort.

Lena knew as well as Kate did that the choice Maeve had given her was no choice at all.

"All right, then, let's get everyone in the same room. I have a few ground rules I need to set before I commit," Lena said with a grim nod. "Might as well do it now and get the tantrum out of the way. It's not like this day can get much worse."

Kate shut the door and trailed after Lena, riding the line between relief and apprehension. She was glad to have her here. Maggie was smart and easy to get along with, but she was also eight years younger than Kate and twelve younger than Lena. They both tended to watch their words and keep their emotions in check around her in an effort not to burden her, the way a mother might with a child.

As for Sasha, she'd practically come out of the womb a full-grown woman in so many ways that it made the age gap feel smaller. But she felt things so deeply that her mood was contagious, which could either be a blessing or a curse. She was a gorgeous Spring afternoon full of sunshine, her bubbling effervescence intoxicating everyone around her, or she was a tornado, dragging everything in her path into that maelstrom of destruction. Sometimes all in one day.

Not Lena, though. Lena was rock steady. It wasn't always good —judgment was swift and often harsh. Criticism was both constructive and plentiful—but you got what you saw. Kate didn't have to guess what Lena would do or think, there were never any surprises.

Almost never, anyway.

She was Kate's contemporary, as well as her port in the storm. Most importantly, she'd be an ally when Kate needed one. And, when Sasha was around, everyone needed an ally at some point or another. When a person was that quick to pop off—quicker than a thought—it was only a matter of time before even the most passive, conflict-resistant person got caught in the crossfire.

But as happy as Kate was that her oldest sister had stuck around, she was also apprehensive. Lena and Sasha were oil and water on their best day, and today certainly wasn't that. No matter how you sliced it, the next few months under the same roof was going to be tough on all of them.

She shoved her worries aside for the moment and stopped in front of the winding staircase. "Mags? Come down when you're done, Lena's here," Kate called.

"Be right down!"

Lena and Kate made their way into the living room where Sasha sat, still looking through pictures.

"Mama and Ma' Mere," she said, a fond smile pulling at her lips. "This one must've been taken after she picked them up from the nuns."

Maeve's mother, a French Canadian beauty named Lorraine, who traveled south to Louisiana just before World War II, had run into tough times with her first husband. When he left her to find work and never came back, she'd brought her two children at that time, Maeve and her brother, Leo, to an orphanage. Once she managed to land herself a factory job and a second husband a year later, she went and got them back so they could be a family again.

Aside from her lifelong staunch refusal to eat canned baked beans after having been fed little else so often as a child of poverty, and a few offhand references about the nuns making her clothes, Maeve rarely spoke of that time in her life. Despite her outwardly matter of fact view of the events, Kate had always felt the experience had broken something in their mother that had never fully healed. As she moved closer to Sasha and examined the picture, she wished now that she'd taken the time to ask more about it. And now it was too late. Such a crying shame that people took all of their memories with them when they died.

Then again, sometimes, maybe it was for the best...

Kate turned away. "How about some tea?" she asked Lena. "Did you eat something?"

Lena nodded. "Étouffée at Crawdad's. I'm good."

"Were you sad they didn't have any avocado toast or whatever it is people eat in Portland?" Sasha asked sweetly. To an outsider, it might've sounded like genuine curiosity, but all three of them knew better.

Lena set her purse on the coffee table and faced their sister with a tight smile.

"First of all, I live in Seattle, as you well know. And second of all, I might have left Louisiana, but I still know good food when I taste it. Can you give it a rest for tonight, Sash? I'm exhausted."

The pitter-patter of footsteps on the stairs stopped the tense conversation short and had Kate blowing out a relieved sigh.

"Maggie is here, so we can hash this out now if you want, Lena."

Maggie swept into the room, auburn curls still damp from the shower, dressed in a pair of boxer shorts and a tank top, fresh-faced and looking far younger than her forty-two years. She wiggled her fingers in Lena's direction. "Hey, sis. I already put up the kitchen, but if you're hungry--"

"She ate," Sasha cut in, back to pretending she was still looking at pictures.

"Oookay, then," Maggie said, plopping into one of the empty chairs beside the coffee table. "What's happening? You staying, Lena? I put fresh sheets in all four bedrooms, just in case."

Kate sat on one side of the couch and Lena took a seat on the other.

"I'll stay, but I have a few requests."

"Naturally," Sasha muttered. "Do go on, *Doctor*."

Kate shook her head and bit back a wry smile. Only Sasha could make that sound like an insult. It really was a wasted talent.

Lena ignored her and pressed on, tucking a strand of silver hair behind one ear. "I've had Alistair email me copies of the will in its entirety, along with the accompanying letters. I've forwarded them to my lawyer to review and check for loopholes." She met each of their gazes in turn. "Make no mistake. If there is a way out of this circus, I'm going to find it."

Sasha fake yawned and set the box of pictures on the floor beside her. "And if there isn't?"

"Then we're stuck here together, aren't we?" Lena said, brows raised. "We'll have to make the best of it. I'm in the middle of a project for my work that I can't just drop on a whim, so I'm going to need sole access to Maeve's study."

"Meaning, you have no plans to, I don't know, help, or anything?" Sasha asked, gesturing around the house with a bitter laugh. "This place is packed from wall to wall with knickknacks and brick-a-brack, dolls and jewelry and clothes and furniture. All thirteen rooms, plus the attic. Three months is about what it's going to take to separate everything out, pick what we want to keep, make a pile to donate, not to mention coordinating a dumpster and the like, getting repairs done so we can sell it, trying to find a realtor. You're just washing your hands of all that...let the peons do it, right?"

"That's not at all what I said, Sash. I just need to make sure I have some time to work and a space to do it. The rest of the time, I'll help with the house."

Kate shot a glance at Lena to gauge how close she was to the edge and was dismayed to find that she was pretty close, but Sasha was too far-gone to realize that she'd breached the danger zone.

"It really has been a long day for us all," Kate cut in smoothly as Maggie tried to disappear into the overstuffed cushions of her chair. "Now that we've heard Lena's concerns, let's all sleep on it, and see how things look in the--"

"What about Mama's funeral?" Sasha demanded, eyes flashing, arms crossed over her heaving chest. "Are you going to help with that?"

"She explicitly expressed to Alistair that she didn't want a funeral or a wake," Lena shot back. "That, when the three months were up, we're to have a party to celebrate her life."

"So that's it? The four of us just are going to pretend she's not dead until then? No private ceremony to say our goodbyes...No nothing? You know, if you ever gave a rat's crack about anyone but yourself, you'd--"

"*Tais-toi!*" Lena thundered. "That's enough of your mouth! You think you're the only one going through something right now?"

Kate was just about to intervene again when the silence was broken by the shattering of glass, followed by the sound of splintering wood, loud as a gunshot. She instinctively covered her face and head with her arms as adrenaline shot through her.

Fear was like a living thing, holding her heart in its icy grip as she tried to make sense of what was happening. But the loud noise was gone as quickly as it had come, and now all she heard was the sound of glass, tinkling against hard wood like a thousand little bells mingling with the sound of her harsh breaths.

She forced her eyes open as she tried to determine what had happened, only to realize she couldn't see a thing because Lena was sprawled over her like a tarp.

"Is everyone okay?" Lena demanded, her voice whip-sharp enough to cut through both the confusion and pounding of blood in Kate's ears.

"Yes...yeah, I'm fine," she croaked as Lena unglued her body from Kate's and stood.

"M-me too," Sasha replied faintly.

Kate turned to find Maggie staring openmouthed at the large object nestled in the pile of wood and decimated glass that had been the coffee table not two feet away from where she was sitting. She pushed herself to her feet and moved toward it, bending closer.

From Kate's vantage point, it looked like a large rock, slightly smaller than a bowling ball, wrapped in white paper.

"Get back, Mags," Lena said as she held up a staying hand and approached the projectile as if it might be a bomb in disguise. "Don't touch it."

Maggie stilled, nostrils flaring as she looked at Lena in panic.

"Did you get hit with any glass?" Lena demanded, searching Maggie's face.

"No. At least, I don't think so," she said as she glanced down at her bare arms and legs, clearly still in shock.

"What the hell is it?" Sasha demanded. True to form, she had transitioned from terrified to furious on a dime, but Kate knew she was as shaken as the rest of them as she glared at the rock.

"It looks like a note," Lena said softly. She bent low, glancing out the shattered window before scooping up the massive stone.

Kate leaned in to get a closer look. Sure enough, bold, blood-red letters stood out against the stark white of the paper used to cover the rock. It was crumpled and misshapen, but one word was clearly legible, written in all capital letters.

Kate swayed in place, suddenly unsteady on her feet, but it didn't matter that her eyes were now closed. The word was stamped on her brain like a fresh tattoo.

MURDERER.

SASHA

"I still can't believe it," Maggie murmured.

The four of them sat around the living room, staring at the note between them like it was a cottonmouth. It had been a half hour since it had come sailing through the window by way of a giant rock and, so far, other than Kate making chamomile tea to "calm everyone's nerves", they'd done nothing about it.

"We need to call the police," Sasha said for what felt like the fiftieth time as she scrubbed a hand over her face in frustration.

Listening to her three sisters go around in circles over what to do next was exhausting, and she could already sense the tension headache building in the back of her neck.

"Someone vandalized Mama's home," she continued. "*Our* home, now. Not to mention that this thing is huge. Unless they used a catapult to launch it, they were close enough to the window to throw it through, meaning they saw us. They saw all of us sitting here and didn't care if they crushed one of our skulls in the process. I don't even understand the debate, here."

"The debate is whether we want to open this can of worms again, Sash," Lena said.

Her calm, even tone only irritated Sasha more.

"Just because you're never around to witness it, doesn't mean it didn't happen, Lena. But I'll break it down for you nice and slow." She inched forward on the velvet, leopard-print armchair she'd been sitting on. "The 'can of worms' was never closed. People have never stopped saying Mama killed Clyde. Sure, they might whisper it now instead of shouting it at her in public like they used to, but the people who thought it back then still think it. That much, I can handle. Who cares what a bunch of jealous, bitter old-timers think? When they start making threats, that's where I draw the line. So I'll give you five more minutes to pull out the big guns and convince me of something different. If not, I'm calling Sheriff Fletcher."

With that, she flopped back, crossing her arms over her chest, one brow raised in a challenge.

"If the Sheriff comes here at ten o'clock at night, the whole town will be flapping about it before breakfast. You know that. Calling is out of the question."

Sasha shot to her feet, her blood pumping now. "Mama may have died, but she certainly didn't make you boss before she did it. I'll call if I want to call."

Lena stood and met her toe to toe. Her green eyes, the color of chipped sea-glass, narrowed and Sasha lifted her chin, refusing to squirm under the weight of her stare. It wasn't easy. The ten years between them felt more like a generation and, while Lena hadn't been around much after she'd left, she'd still practically raised all three of them when they were small.

But that was then. They were equals now, whether Lena thought so or not.

None of those affirmations stopped the flutter of fear in her heart as Lena stood over her, a trembling finger pointed in Sasha's face.

"Listen to me, you selfish little brat. If you want your piece of this place, the four of us are stuck here for the foreseeable future. Now, that might not affect your shifts at the diner one town over, or put a wrench in your plans to screw your way through the rest of the parish before you give up the ghost, but it's not so convenient for everyone else. I'm using three of the final four months of my sabbatical, that was meant to be spent on indigenous women's studies, stuck here in La Pierre instead, and I'm livid about it. So sit down, shut your trap, and let the grownups talk."

The words hit like razor blades, each one a new cut, and Sasha had to take a second to absorb them all.

"Lena...seriously, that's not helping," Kate murmured, wincing.

Desperate for a release, Sasha turned her impotent fury on Kate, who was a much easier target. "You know what, Holly Hobby? I don't need you to defend me all the time. I can handle myself. Besides, what can she do to me? I'm too old to whoop, and even if I wasn't, Pacific Northwest Lena is far too refined and citified to do it. Anyway, she'd probably throw out her back or break a h-"

It was the slap heard around the world. Or, at least, when Lena's hand connected with Sasha's cheek, it sure felt that way.

"You're never too old to whoop, little miss," Lena shot back, eyes glittering. "Remember that."

Part of Sasha, albeit one that was real, real deep down at the moment, was kind of impressed. Maybe old Lena wasn't as dead inside as she seemed.

But the part that had spent a lifetime wishing for her big sister's approval? Was gutted. Shame and regret and anger swirled together, making an oily soup in her belly.

She wanted to lash out, maybe even slap her back, but she couldn't seem to get her hand to work. What would it prove, anyway? Nothing was going to change the fact that the one person on this entire earth who had truly understood her...who really *saw* her, was dead.

The anger drained away in a rush as her throat went tight and achy, and her eyes filled with tears.

"Sash, I'm sorry," Lena said, stepping closer, hand extended. "I was totally out of line..."

She couldn't get the words out, but if she could have, she'd have told Lena that none of that was important. Not the argument. Not the slap. Not the rock through the window, or the note.

The only thing that mattered was that their mama was gone.

And this time, unlike so many others, she wasn't coming back...

MAGGIE

It didn't happen every time the four of them were together, but it happened most times. The moment where Maggie was reminded that she was different. Not a bad different—at least, not all the time—but different just the same.

Lena would never have slapped her like that. Not when she was little, and certainly not now. Then again, she'd only gotten to live with her for a couple years before Lena had left La Pierre for good. Even after Maggie's birth mother passed away and she'd moved into the house with them, Lena had treated Maggie like a beloved little cousin. She'd carry her around on her hip while she cooked them pancake breakfasts and absently ruffle her hair when she passed by. Not at all the way she treated Kate, who seemed more like a trusted friend, or Sasha, who Lena did her best to rein in like a wild horse in need of breaking.

Maggie had loved her relationship with Lena when she was a child. As she grew older, though, it only served as a reminder that, while Lena viewed her as an honored member of the family, she would never be her sister.

Some days, it bothered her. Not today, though. Today, she was happy for the buffer it offered.

"I sent a message to the Sheriff's Office."

Lena was still staring at the empty space where Sasha had been before rushing out of the room in tears, and she turned toward Maggie, blinking in confusion.

"What?"

Maggie swallowed hard and forced the words out a second time. "When you were all arguing. They have a tip line that accepts text messages. I sent one to them. Someone will be here any minute."

Lena squeezed her eyes closed and barked out a laugh. "Oh, for crying out--"

"I'm sorry, but if we don't do anything about it, we'll be targets for the next three months."

Kate and Lena shared a loaded look, and Lena turned away with a sigh.

"Thanks a lot, Maggie. Now the whole town is going to know about it by morning. I was just thinking to myself, 'Well, at least it can't get worse', and you've proven me wrong."

"All right, there's nothing to do about it now. What's done is done," Kate said, ever the peacemaker. Maggie could tell she was as upset as Lena. She was just better at pretending.

"It's nothing they haven't said before, anyway. We don't want people thinking they can come and do that type of stuff just because Mama isn't alive to stop them, or it will never end," Maggie said, more firmly this time. There was no doubt Maeve herself had been a big deterrent, even in her later years. She had a lot of questionable connections from her riverboat casino and whiskey running days. Plus, her hands may have been twisted with arthritis, but she could still pull the trigger on Old Betty and pepper someone's keister with buckshot if the need arose, and wouldn't have hesitated a lick to do it.

The thought had a smile tugging at her lips and her chest going tight with emotion.

She couldn't get derailed thinking about their mother's death right now. She had to focus on her legacy, and part of that was making sure people didn't get away with running around calling Maeve Blanchard a murderer. She was a lot of things, but never that.

"Besides, we might as well all ingratiate ourselves with the Sheriff, now that we'll be here awhile. You know what Mama always said..."

"'Keep your friends close, and local law enforcement closer'," Sasha finished for her as she stepped into the living room again before shooting a shamefaced glance toward Lena. "I think I still just can't quite believe she's gone...it's hitting me hard."

That was as close to an apology as Maggie had ever heard come from Sasha, and apparently Lena agreed, because she nodded.

"I know."

Good enough.

"Maeve's got a lot of stuff here to get through. Boxes from as far back as the sixties full of business documents and paperwork. We've got to remember that some of it wasn't even close to legal. We just don't want to invite the cops in more than we have to, is all. All right?" Kate said, leveling Maggie with a long look.

She nodded and was about to answer when a knock sounded at the door.

"Let's get this over with," she said, running a hand through her dark hair as she went to answer it.

Low voices murmured in the foyer and, a moment later, Kate returned, leading a man in his late thirties with freckles and ginger hair along with her. His large, gray hat was in his hand and he was dressed in a snappy police uniform, a gleaming star on his chest that read Deputy Rutledge.

He gave each of them a nod in turn. "Maggie, Miss Lena... Sasha," he said, cheeks going ruddy as he met Sasha's gaze.

"Rusty," Sasha said with a crooked half-smile. "How's your mama an' them?"

"Everybody's fine, thanks," he returned, looking anywhere but at Sasha now. "I was so sorry to learn about Maeve. She'll be missed." They each murmured their thanks before he continued. "I hear there was some trouble tonight?"

Maggie stood and gestured to the destroyed table. "Someone threw a rock through the window with this note attached." She held it up for inspection.

Someone's gotta pay, one way or another. MURDERER.

He hitched a hand on his hip and nodded slowly as he took it from her hand. "How long ago?"

"Right before Maggie messaged the department," Lena replied. "Not sure what time."

"We'll have that on file, for sure. I was at a domestic call over on Dupont Road, so I beat Sheriff Fletcher here, but he isn't far behind. When he gets here, he'll ask y'all some questions while I'll take a look around outside and see what I see."

Like he'd conjured him with words, a second knock sounded on the door and, a moment later, it opened.

"It's Joe, can I come in?"

"Come on," Kate called, turning toward the foyer with a wave. "Hey, Joe."

The Sheriff stepped in the room, hat in hand. "Kate, Maggie, Sasha..." His lean face remained impassive, dark gray eyes unreadable as he looked over and locked gazes with Lena. "Good to see you, Lena. Been a long time."

"You too, Joe."

Maggie flicked a glance between the Sheriff and her oldest sister. She hadn't been surprised to see the interplay between Rusty and Sasha. Lena had been harsh when she'd accused Sasha of sleeping her way through La Pierre and the surrounding towns, but she hadn't been exactly wrong. Plus, Rusty was handsome in an "aw shucks" kind of way, and fit squarely into Sasha's thirty-to-sixty acceptable age bracket. It stood to reason she'd treated the boy to a tumble at one point or another. If she knew her sister, it only had to happen once and he'd be blushing like that when he saw her for the rest of their lives. It was the electric current between Sheriff Joe and Lena that was doing Maggie's head in...

Had prim and proper schoolmarm Lena taken the rugged Sheriff for a spin on one of her rare visits to La Pierre, at some point? The thought of Lena living a little actually lifted her spirits some. She made a mental note to ask Sasha about it later.

"I was real sorry to hear about your mama," he said, his smooth baritone low and soothing.

Sasha sidled up and slipped her arms around the Sheriff's waist, tucking her head into his broad shoulder.

"It's been tough, Sheriff, but we're getting through," she said with a sigh. He gave her an awkward pat and then took a step back.

"Glad to hear it. Now what's this about a vandal and a threat?"

Kate and Lena took the reins and walked both lawmen through the order of events. Rusty furiously took notes on a little white notepad as the Sheriff listened carefully.

"So nothing strange before that. No noise from outside, anything like that?" he asked when they'd finished.

"No. We were...talking and then the rock came crashing through the window," Kate said with a shrug.

"Do you remember hearing a car starting, tires squealing, or seeing headlights afterward?"

Lena and Kate looked at each other, then toward Maggie and Sasha.

"Not that I recall," Lena said.

"We were all pretty startled, but I think I would've noticed," Kate added, frowning. "The porch lights were off, and the headlights would've been noticeable through the picture window, unless they kept them off."

"I didn't hear a car," Maggie piped in, thinking back to that moment. "I'd have remembered because the sound of all the critters got a lot louder once the window was shattered. Like someone turned up the volume outside. That's what my brain was focused on in the moment, for some reason."

The Sheriff glanced at the window. Kate had covered it with plastic wrap and tape shortly after it had happened, but the sound from outside was still amplified.

"I agree. I'm guessing they were on foot," Sasha said.

"Which means it was someone who lives close, or they had a car parked nearby," the Sheriff murmured, turning his attention toward Sasha. "Anyone you can think of that might be behind this? I know it's not the first time Maeve has dealt with something like this, but it's been a long time. And I don't recall a threat in the past."

Sasha lived just fifteen minutes away and had spent the most time with Maeve in the past few years, so it made sense to ask her specifically, but Maggie couldn't deflect the stab of guilt.

She lived just an hour away and had only managed to make it to visit a few times a year. As a freelance marketing specialist who made her own hours, she could've done better.

She *should've* done better.

"No one, specifically," Sasha said after thinking for a long moment. "Of course, Mama pissed off a few of the ladies in town, as you know. Their husbands were always sniffing around her back in the day and they're jealous old biddies holding a grudge. And she's mouthed off to more politicians and the like than probably anyone in La Pierre. But I don't think any of them would stoop to this level. Especially not now. She's an institution in this town."

"If we're all assuming what we're assuming, that whoever did this was referring to Clyde's death, then maybe one of his family members is trying to kick up some dust," Maggie said with a shrug. "Seems like a strange thing to bring up thirty-odd years later, but who can say?"

"Good enough," he said, tipping his chin at Rusty. "I'm sure whoever did this is long gone, but I'm going to take a look around outside. Why don't you bag and tag the stone and the note, then head out to the barn and get some plywood to cover the window nice and tight until they can get someone out here to replace it. Come morning, first thing, give a call to the Jensens next door and ask if they saw or heard anything around the time of the incident."

Their neighbors were fifty acres or more away, so it was unlikely, but Rusty inclined his head and tugged his flashlight from his belt as he headed off to do the Sheriff's bidding.

"Don't hesitate to call if you think of anything else at all or have any more trouble, all right?" the Sheriff asked, tugging a business card out of his pocket and extending it in the general direction of where Lena and Kate were standing.

It was Sasha who plucked it from his fingers with a nod, though. "Thanks, Sheriff. We feel much safer already, knowing you're on the case."

He lifted a hand and made his way back to the foyer. "I'll be in touch."

"I wish," Sasha murmured under her breath as she watched him go. The second he was out of sight, she fanned herself with the card like she was having a fit of the vapors. "That man is just a tall drink of water, and every time I see him, I feel thirsty."

"Yeah, well, we don't need him poking around here for any reason at all, so find yourself a water fountain and cool off a little," Lena said, dropping into an armchair with a sigh. This time, her words were lighter than before, and Sasha let them roll off with a wink.

It was only when the lawmen had gone an hour later that the last of the adrenaline drained away and Maggie realized how exhausted she was. By the time she trudged upstairs, she was dead on her feet, sure she'd sleep like a log.

Instead, she dreamed of bloody notes and broken glass and murder.

MAEVE

January 7th, 1965

My Dearest Maeve,

I'm writing to let you know that I'm through with my training and I'm set to be sent over to Vietnam, though they haven't yet told me where, exactly. I'll do my best to call before I go. It's been a tough few months without you and I have taken to looking at my picture of you every night before sleeping. It gives me strength to keep going. I am eager to return home and I wish I didn't enlist for such a long term. Four years seems like an eternity that would've been better spent with you.

We've been told that there will be no leave during our tour of duty, so it will still be longer than a year until we can see each other again. Knowing that, I have taken to counting the days 'til I get to see your pretty face in person.

Tell me about what you've been up to and how things are going back home? I was so sorry to hear about Annalise's condition taking a turn for the worse. Could you check in on them for me and make sure Harry is really doing all right? He never was one to complain. If they seem in a bad way, try to give him some of the money without making too much of a fuss about it. He likely won't take it but it's worth a try. I've been sending as much as I can and I hope it's enough so you can quit that job at the market, even if we need to give some to the Seplaskys. I would hate for you to have to work your pretty little fingers to the bone.

Please know that I am thinking of you always, my love. Keep enjoying life and don't worry too much about me. I'll take care of myself just fine and it'll still likely be months before I see any combat.

All my love,

Ollie

January 21st, 1965

Maeve, my love,

I wrote as soon as I got your letter but there will likely be some delay because I am overseas now. I was excited to hear that you quit your job at the market. I'm happy you found a use for those peach trees in the backyard but make sure you're careful, I couldn't bear for my lovely wife to be stuck in prison over money that we won't need as soon as I'm home.

Keep checking in on Harry and Annalise, and try to make it a regular thing to give him a bit of cash when he'll take it. I'm glad to hear that you've been bringing food for him and Annalise. I know she appreciates it even if she can't do much in the way of expressing it right now. It puts me at ease to know that you're all there taking care of each other while I'm away.

That box of photos you sent me with the letter has done more than you know for my morale. Though it's no substitute for your touch, they make me remember what I'm doing all this for. With your next care package, I'd love for you to send me a few of those toffees that Old Russell makes, I've had a hankering for one. I set aside a little extra money for you this month so you could buy yourself the next pretty dress you see in the window of Bonnie's shop. When you do, I'd love to see a picture of you wearing it.

Always yours,

Ollie

February 19th, 1965

Sweet Maeve,

Sorry it took so long to get back, we've been very busy but I replied as soon as I could. I can hardly believe those numbers from your new business venture. For the first time, I'm mighty thankful that La Pierre is still a dry parish! Don't feel the need to pull in more dough than you're already making, though, it's not worth getting caught. It will be hard to have the reunion like we *planned if you're in the slammer. I am sure glad you're making enough to afford to buy some nice things for yourself. Speaking of nice things, that dress you picked out suits you perfectly. I keep your picture with me always and jealousy has just about turned all the fellas here against me.*

Every time I eat one of those toffees you sent, I think of how I felt the first time I saw you in Old Russell's store. I had planned to ration them out but I've been through near two-dozen already and I fear I'll run out before next week's end.

My affection for you grows even here and the boys have taken to calling me Loverboy because of how often I speak of you. It was quiet in our area for a while but there have been a few attacks lately. Not too many casualties so far. I haven't been in much danger as of yet and I've been more afraid of dying of boredom than battle, so don't worry about me, all right?

Every day without being able to hold you in my arms has been hell and I regret enlisting every time I look at your picture. I would love to help you in your moonshining when I get back home.

Keep holding down the fort until I return. I'll write back when I can and make sure you don't get too bogged down in working and have fun once in a while, my sweet.

With love,

Ollie

March 5th, 1965

. . .

Dear Ollie,

I sent some more of those toffees you like, along with another set of pictures, I think you'll like these ones even more than the last ones. I can hardly imagine how tough it must be to be deprived of my feminine charms and company for such a long period. In seriousness, I think of you often and am eager to see you when your tour is over.

My business is going well, with more locals coming to me for liquor. I sold a few hundred dollars' worth so far this month and I expect to make more in the weeks to come. I've been putting a lot of hours in so you won't have to re-enlist after your service is over. By the way, I don't need to worry about going to the slammer. Sheriff Jacobs and his deputies appreciate a case of free moonshine as much as the next fella.

I've been giving Harry some odd jobs to do, so as to not hurt his pride too much, but I've been providing for him well enough and I'm trying to convince him to quit his job so he has more time to take care of Annalise. He insists that he doesn't want to rely on us but I'll update if there is progress on that front.

Enjoy the photographs and toffee that I sent for you, I'll keep sending some every few weeks so you won't have to eat them so sparingly. Don't get yourself injured or worse out there, I can't wait to see you early next year when your first tour is over. Hopefully I'll be able to give you a taste of the life of comfort that I'm trying to build for us for when your four years are over.

Goodbye for now,

Maeve

. . .

March 16th, 1965

Dear Ollie,

I'm sure you've been busy and just haven't had time to reply, but I figured I'd send you another package with some more toffees and a few updates. My business has grown further and I've enclosed a few pictures of me in some choice dresses I've purchased lately, in a scheme to get the entirety of the marine corps jealous over your beautiful wife.

I've been making new changes at our house every week and you're going to love our garage, which I have turned into an area for your woodworking projects that you love so much. I hope you're doing well and that I am still in your thoughts.

Write back when you're able,

Maeve

May 16th, 1965

To My Dearest Ollie,

This will be the eighth letter I've sent since your last reply and I am beginning to become frantic. My fears grow with each day.

Have you went off with another woman and started a family? Are you missing? Are you dead? I can think of little else these days. I sit by the door waiting for the mail to arrive each morning and I pray each night for your safe return before crying myself to sleep.

I cannot bear this much longer, my love, please write to me, even if it's just to let me know that you're alive.

Your loving wife,

Maeve

LENA

Dust sparkled in the sunbeams streaming in from the slatted windows as Lena carefully folded the crinkled, yellowed paper. She slid it back into its faded envelope and placed that on top of a stack next to her feet, all marked Return to Sender. Reaching for the last in the box, her knuckles again brushed the old photo precariously perched on the corner. A faint smile tugged at her lips as she picked it up, instead. She simply couldn't resist gazing at the face there one more time.

Dark hair, shorn in a military buzz cut, still gave the impression of wild disarray somehow. The uniform jacket appeared slightly too big in the shoulders for such a young, slender man, and slightly too short at the waist. His blue eyes twinkled with good humor, perhaps even more so than his big, goofy grin. Lena always wondered what he had been laughing at during the shot. Her mother had told her of the legendary jokes and pranks they'd pulled on one another during their short time together. This one must have been good.

One finger stroked the celluloid features. She'd never been able to resist the old photos as a little girl, and time hadn't changed that fact.

"Hello, Ollie Daddy," she murmured, reverting to the name she'd called him in her mind as a child.

She was under no delusions. He hadn't fathered her; she'd done the math. The fantasy that had spawned the secret nickname lasted until she realized he'd been in Vietnam when Maeve had gotten pregnant with her, and had never come back. She still remembered that bitter realization, the day of her eighth birthday party. She'd bawled for an hour in her room while four-year-old Kate threw a crying fit of her own about the birthday cake they'd all had to wait to eat because of Lena's crying.

Kate's tears had made for a good cover; Maeve had never known just how difficult her eldest took the loss of Ollie as her daddy. Not that her mother had ever told her he was. She'd done a lot of things in her day, but Maeve wasn't much on lying. It wouldn't have mattered. Turned out, the following year, her classmates started doing some math themselves. They made sure she never forgot what she was.

What she'd never realized was that she wasn't the only one suffering Ollie's loss. Maeve had always been such a tough cookie, soldiering through whatever life threw her way. The depth of her grief was plain in those letters, and it weighed heavy on Lena's heart.

She shoved the photo on the bottom of the box and placed the accompanying letters atop, making a mental note to share them with her sisters later that day. She sat back, sweeping the gray tendrils that had fallen out of her bun back atop her head. They clung to her neck, refusing to stay in place.

"It's hot as hell up here," she muttered, giving up. She nudged the box into place with one foot and stood. She'd been up since dawn and it was past time for breakfast.

Heading down the ladder, Lena decided to head to a café to pick up coffee and beignets for everyone. It would be as much of a peace offering as a bribe.

Lena frowned as she made her way to the kitchen. Why the hell would Maggie want to involve the entire town in their family's business? Sasha would do it just to be contrary, but Maggie—

"Mornin'."

Kate sat at the kitchen table, upright as a primrose, sipping from a steaming cup.

"Morning." She hadn't spent any quality time in person with her sister in... she couldn't remember how long. Besides, they had to discuss a few things that might be better done in private. "Had anything to eat yet?" Lena asked as she stepped into the kitchen.

"Not yet. I thought I'd fix some egg whites," Kate brought the cup to her nose and inhaled, "in a bit."

"Egg whites?" Lena wrinkled her nose. "Boring. Come on. We're going to the café."

"We are?"

"Where else are we going to get the beignets we so desperately need?" Lena swiped her keys from the board and jingled them.

"Nowhere," Kate said with a grin. "Obviously."

The two didn't say anything as they walked out to the car. A day that had started out warm had turned into a virtual steam bath as the sun rose, burning off the morning dew.

Lena had forgotten this part about living in La Pierre. It got so hot that the air felt like soup, and she wondered what it was like in Seattle right now.

Probably perfect.

"So," Kate said once they had settled in the car, cranked up the air and started driving, "Joe seemed particularly happy to see you were back in town." She studied her sister intently.

Lena glanced at her out of the corner of her eye, but kept her attention on the road in front of her. La Pierre had never had many joggers, to her memory, especially this time of year, but things could have changed in—Lena winced and put the specific number out of her head—the intervening years.

"Yes, he always was nice," Lena said warily.

"I remember you guys were friendly in high school before you left," Kate said, her tone almost too casual.

"Stop," Lena said as she approached a traffic light.

"Stop what?" Kate asked with an innocent shrug.

"I think you have a point to make so why don't you just make it?" Bringing the car to a full stop at the light, she turned to frown at her sister.

"What point would I be making?"

"Katherine Fontuna--"

"Smith," Kate corrected.

"Katherine Smith, just say what you're going to say or stop talking about it altogether. I'm not getting any younger here."

Kate glanced down and shrugged. "Joe just seemed rather taken with you and I wondered how you felt about him back then."

Lena stared at her sister, then turned abruptly to face the front.

"You're asking about romance, *now*? We're here packing up Maeve's house, I don't want to be here at all, someone threw a rock through our window, and this seems like the time for this conversation?" She gripped the wheel more tightly, already bitterly regretting her decision to invite her sister along. "Besides, Sasha is the one who seems interested."

Kate let out a snort. "Sasha wants every man. It's not personal." She paused. "Well, maybe it is in this case. I think she was flirting because he's paying you the attention she thinks should be hers. And, you're avoiding the subject. Which means..."

Lena glanced at her sister to find Kate grinning at her.

"You like him!"

Lena rolled her eyes, refusing to dignify that with a response.

Kate cackled in glee as Lena eased the car through the intersection.

"I swear, you're twelve years old sometimes. But now that you've gotten that out of your system, can we talk about the elephant in the room? I still can't believe Sasha wanted to bring the police into all this," Lena said, deftly changing the subject.

"She doesn't understand what this could do to our family," Kate said, shaking her head. "She's acting out of anger, not thought."

"She's acting out of spite."

It was Kate's turn to roll her eyes. "We could be in danger," she pointed out.

"Don't defend her."

"Lena, she does have a point."

Lena snorted.

"If she didn't, Maggie wouldn't have texted the police."

"She has no idea the mess she's causing. All Maeve's dirty laundry will be aired all over again. The bootlegging, racketeering, not to mention Clyde."

Kate nodded, her expression growing shuttered.

"No one wants to mention Clyde. And Maeve was wild, but she was an institution in this town. I don't want anyone besmirching that, and I don't think Maggie does, either. She just agrees with Sasha that we could be in danger, and she thinks if we let people start nonsense like this and do nothing about it, it will escalate. Who knows? Maybe she's right."

Lena scowled.

"That rock could easily have cracked one of our heads open," Kate hurried on. "Do you want your sisters to get hurt?"

"You know I don't. But we can handle our own business. We don't need anyone else poking around. Certainly not the cops. I'm sure it was just a one-off. Typical small town nonsense." Lena indicated the townsfolk with a wave of one hand.

"What if it wasn't?"

Lena glanced at her. "Next time they might have better aim. And it's not like we have a choice. Joe is already involved and I don't think he's just going to let this go. It is what it is."

"At least you'll get to see him again." Kate nudged her elbow.

Lena blew out a long-suffering sigh. Despite the topic of conversation, she had to admit it was nice being with Kate in person. They spoke on the phone, Kate flew out to see her every so often, and vice versa, and every time Lena was reminded of just how much she loved spending time with her sister. If only they didn't have to be in La Pierre to do it.

The two let quiet settle between them, a comfortable silence. It didn't take long to get to the café. Even so, Lena felt surprised at the nostalgia that washed over her as she turned down the main street after being gone so long.

"At least we don't have to walk far," Kate said as they stepped out of the car and shut their doors. "Parking can be hell this time of day."

"You just hate the heat," Lena shot back. "Maybe you should have brought a dainty little parasol."

Kate just glared at her.

Downtown was busier than Lena remembered, especially at this time of day. The two of them crossed the street, chatting as they approached Beignet Parfait.

"Isn't it funny?" Lena asked. "We haven't been here in decades. But as soon as we decide to pick up beignets, we just wordlessly head here."

"It's not like we had any other choice." Kate gestured as if to say 'obviously'. "It's Beignet Parfait or that place over on Third--"

"You shut your mouth," Lena hissed. "That place on Third has doughnuts. *Not* beignets."

"You still hate it," Kate chuckled, "after all this time."

"I will die on this hill!" Lena shook her fist in the air before turning toward her sister.

Then, she looked past Kate, her smile widening.

"Well," Kate chuckled softly, "look at that. Apparently, we aren't the only ones out enjoying a nice beignet."

There, walking down the sidewalk, came Sheriff Joe Fletcher. He held a small white bag in one hand and licked powdered sugar off of his fingers.

Kate wasn't wrong about one thing. Joe Fletcher was a fine looking man. It was a shame he didn't live somewhere other than her own personal hell.

Sheriff Joe nodded as he closed the gap between them. "Mornin', ladies." He smiled at them both but his eyes lingered on Lena, a fact that she was sure Kate would note.

She felt her cheeks heating as she glanced down, berating herself. *You're not a schoolgirl, Lena. Get it together.*

"I planned to call the house today, actually," he said.

"Oh?" She looked up at him again, worried that he could hear her heart race. This couldn't be good.

"I just wanted you ladies to know," he said, his tone dropping low, "I have a lead on your vandal that I'm hoping will pan out in the next few days."

Lena's heart sank as Kate nodded.

"You don't need..." Lena stumbled, not quite certain what to say. "That is, we don't want to be any trouble."

"Absolutely no trouble at all," Sheriff Joe assured her. "I know how important it is for y'all to put this business to rest."

"Yes," Lena said with a firm nod. "That's what we want, to just put all this to rest and move on."

"I'll keep you posted when I hear. It's...it's real nice seeing you in La Pierre again." He smiled, a bit of boyish charm in his grin. "Even under these circumstances, I'm glad you came home."

"Thank you." Lena blinked, not quite knowing what to say. "I'm... I'm surprised to find I actually missed it in some ways."

"Oh me, too," Kate interjected. "I'm very surprised."

This time, yes, Lena felt certain that his gaze lingered on her.

"That's just wonderful." Kate's smile was even wider now. "Isn't it, Lena? Good to know Sheriff Joe has everything under control?"

"It sure is," Lena responded flatly.

"Anyway, I'll be in touch real soon." He stood up straighter and tipped his head in a curt nod. "This is a priority for me, until we get things resolved."

"Good," Lena said. "Just great."

"Thank you, Sheriff," Kate chimed in. "We'll both look forward to talking to you very soon."

Sheriff Joe nodded at them and then continued on his way.

"You are a terrible sister," Lena muttered from the side of her mouth.

"I'm the best sister." Kate shot her a sly glance. "A terrible sister would have told him that you have the hots for him."

She was right on that score. But despite the fact that she could see the levity in the situation, she couldn't shake her concern about Sheriff Joe being hot on the trail of their vandal.

Something deep in her bones told her they'd all be better off not knowing...

KATE

What temperature does the oven have to be on?

Kate stared down at the text lighting her phone and tapped out a quick response.

350 for 20 minutes.

She'd left a sheet of paper with all the proper heating instructions for each meal on the counter, but God forbid Frank bother himself to read it. Apparently, it was easier for him to text her and ask.

Of the twenty-plus texts she'd gotten over the three days since she'd been gone, exactly none of them had been about her. He hadn't asked how she was holding up after Maeve's death, or about how her sisters were, or if there was anything he could do to make things easier.

The only indication that he even remembered her mother had passed away was his question about the inheritance.

Jerk.

Won't the plastic wrap melt if I put it in the oven?

She had half a mind to type back, "No", just to see what happened next, but restrained herself. After all, it was hardly his fault. Frank was Frank. The same now as he'd been when she'd run off to marry him at nineteen. Selfish. Lazy. Indifferent. But he was there. Constant. She didn't have to worry if he'd run off or cheat. He would never put in the time or the effort. He'd been a decent father, so long as most of his interaction with the kids happened from his well-worn seat on the couch.

No, her recent irritation wasn't on Frank. It was on her. She was the one who needed the attitude adjustment. He'd kept up his side of the bargain, and she needed to keep up hers.

You need to take the plastic off, dear.

"Everything all right back home?" Lena asked as she settled back into the seat across from Kate.

They'd already eaten a beignet and worked their way through a cup of coffee apiece, and Lena had gone for a refill.

"Yeah, Frank's just a little out of sorts trying to figure out how to manage on his own," Kate said with a forced smile. "Once we get into a routine, it will be fine. The first week will just be an adjustment for him."

Lena's eyes narrowed. "Mmm, like a kindergartner's first day at school," she said before taking a sip from her freshly topped off coffee mug.

"Come on, Lena, give it a rest," Kate groaned, flipping her phone face down in case Frank continued to pepper her with ludicrous questions.

"What? I'm just saying, he's like a giant infant. It's nothing you don't already know."

"You haven't even seen him in almost ten years. How would you know?"

"Whenever we talk on the phone, he interrupts at least five times. You've trained him to be as helpless as a one-legged dog. I'm surprised the man can even dress himself," she added with a snort.

Kate tried to keep her expression neutral as she reached for another beignet.

"Oh my God, he can't, can he?" Lena demanded, flopping back into her seat like she'd been hit by a sniper. "You lay out his clothes for him, don't you?" she asked incredulously.

"He's color blind, is all," Kate said, realizing how silly it sounded even when she said it. "It's just easier if I do it."

"Easier for who? Do you wipe his bottom after he makes a number two, as well, then?"

Kate wanted to stay irritated, but a laugh bubbled from her lips and some of the tension drained out of her. What was good for the goose was good for her sister, apparently, and she'd done her fair share of yanking Lena's chain today.

It felt good to have her here now. Right, somehow, despite her differences with Maeve. Something told her their mother was smiling down on them right now, watching.

"That's ridiculous. I draw the line at clipping his toenails," she teased back.

"Lord a' mercy," Lena said, covering her mouth. "I think I just threw up a little. Please tell me you're kidding."

"I'm kidding. But I get it. You're way too much of a feminist to cook and freeze meals for your man while you're away. I don't mind, though, so can we talk about something else, please?"

"If you didn't mind, you wouldn't look like you just ate a lemon every time you looked at your phone," Lena said, her smile fading. "Kate, I know it didn't feel like an option before when the kids were young, or once Frank stopped working and money was so tight. But once we sell the house..."

"I'm not talking about this right now," she replied, meeting her sister's all-too perceptive gaze. "Cease fire."

Lena opened her mouth and then closed it with a snap, sending a shudder of relief through Kate. She didn't know what made her say it...the phrase the two of them had come up with as kids to ensure they never said anything they'd regret to one another. The fact that Lena not only remembered it, but had held to the rules of their decades-old treaty—struck in the dark of night after a bitter fight over a baby-doll—set off an emotional chain reaction inside Kate that had her blinking back tears.

"I love you, no matter what," Lena said, breaking the silence. "Now, we'd better get back before Sasha gets mad and burns the house down or something."

While she had her big sister in such a cuddly mood...

"Speaking of, I really do think you can cut her some slack. I know the two of you don't see eye to eye, but she's trying her best."

For the second time in as many minutes, Lena didn't argue. To Kate's surprise, she just inclined her head. Her brain was still churning to come up with something else to get out of Lena while she was feeling so charitable when a shadow fell over the table.

"Katie, me darlin' girl. Lena..."

Kate looked up with a start and then shot to her feet. "Uncle Harry!" She wrapped her arms around the old man and squeezed, hard.

He returned her embrace with the same enthusiasm and held on tight, his chest quaking against Kate's ribs. They stayed like that for a while until he sucked in a quavering breath and pulled away.

His eyes were bloodshot and he was carrying a few extra pieces of luggage under each eye, so there was no point in asking how he was doing. It was written all over his grief-stricken face.

"Harry," Lena said, getting to her feet and leaning in for a hug.

Harry gripped her in a tight, albeit briefer, embrace and then stepped back. "Let me get a look at you," he managed, his voice husky. "As beautiful as I remember," he said, patting her cheek with a gnarled hand. "Glad you were able to come home for this. I know your mama would be thrilled."

Kate could feel her sister bristling at the word "home" but to her credit, she didn't correct him.

"There's a lot of work to be done," she said diplomatically. "I was so sorry to hear about Annalise's passing."

"I appreciate that, and the flowers you sent were beautiful. I think she was ready to go for a long time, by that point. It was me who wasn't ready. Never easy," he added, pursing his lips. "Can I buy you girls a coffee or something?"

"We're actually just finishing up but I was going to call you this evening," Kate said, laying a gentle hand on his frail shoulder. "We'd love if you could come by for supper...maybe day after tomorrow? That will give us some time to clean up the house a bit and get situated."

Harry's milky green eyes lit up and he nodded. "Yes, I'd like that a lot. What time should I be there?"

She could feel Lena's stare but she ignored her. "Around five o'clock. We can reminisce and have a nice whiskey sour on the porch, first."

"Perfect. I have some things of your mama's I wanted to give to you girls anyway."

"We'll see you then," Kate said with a kind smile.

He tottered away, leaving her and Lena alone again.

"With as much as we have to do on that relic of a house, you really think we have time to be throwing dinner parties?" Lena asked, her voice a whisper but still somehow sounding like a shout. "I'm here for two months and twenty-nine more days. Whatever isn't done, isn't done, and y'all are going to have to deal with it."

Kate almost smiled at that, wondering if Lena realized how often she slipped out of her fancy school, transcontinental accent when she was angry. Maybe Kate would tell her one day and she'd try to be a little less angry all the time...

"Maeve asked us to check in on him and make sure he was all right, and that's what we're going to do."

Lena looked like she was about to continue arguing, but when

Kate met her gaze head on and crossed her arms over her chest, she went quiet.

Kate didn't put her foot down often, but when she did, she put it ankle deep in cement. She wasn't budging, and Lena knew it.

"Fine, well, if we're doing a supper, we're doing a low-country boil. I haven't had one since last time I was here."

Kate smiled, happy to compromise on that front.

The note and the Sheriff's words momentarily forgotten, the two paid their bill and began making a grocery list as they headed out to the car.

As she slipped into the passenger's seat, she caught sight of Harry standing on the corner talking to Pastor West. The good man of God had his arm around Harry, clearly offering words of comfort, and Kate found her throat going tight again.

She and her mother had their issues—most people in close contact with Maeve would say the same—but they'd been close. She felt like she'd gotten to a point where she'd at least understood her mother and her choices in life, and loved her in spite of some of the worst ones.

But Harry had accepted Maeve for everything she was. Completely, without reservation. They were the best of friends, since before even Lena was born, and they'd surely been more over the years, in between Maeve's many marriages and lovers, and Annalise's debilitating medical crises that required all of Harry's attention, some years more than others.

How much different all of their lives would have been if Maeve had met Harry before she'd married Ollie...before Harold met Annalise? She wouldn't have had to mourn the death of a husband at the age of twenty. She wouldn't have spent her whole life desperately in search of a husband as devoted to her as Harry was to Annalise.

And she wouldn't have married Clyde McFadden, who had ruined everything.

SASHA

Sasha plugged one last forkful of potatoes into her mouth and blew out a happy sigh.

"That was something special, y'all. I'm glad I wore my leggings because, if not, I think I would've popped some buttons," she said with a grin as she set her utensils on her clean plate.

"You ladies really outdid yourselves," Harry said with a nod of thanks. "I can't remember enjoying a meal more than this one."

"Certainly not one Mama cooked for you, Uncle Harry," Sasha added with a chuckle.

Everyone around the table joined her as Harry shook his head ruefully. "She tried, bless her heart. It was nineteen seventy-seven, twelve years after she started sending casseroles over for me and Annalise each week, that I finally got up the gumption to tell her the truth."

"Which was?" Kate asked with a grin.

"We fed them to the pigs. And the real kicker?" he added,

wheezing with laughter. "Half the time they wouldn't even eat them."

Even Lena, who had been stone-faced for the first half of the evening, had to laugh at that one. Over the next half hour, they all traded stories about Maeve Blanchard's notoriously questionable cooking skills. It was only when they'd finished their dessert of sweet potato pie that the laughter died down and Harry's face grew troubled.

"Maeve was no chef, but she's done a lot of good in this town. I was troubled to hear that you all had an issue the other night...care to fill me in?"

Sasha wiped her mouth with the fussy cloth napkin and then tossed it on the table. "It's probably nothing. Some kids wanting to cause trouble or something, but I'd hoped they'd have found out who did it by now. It's been days."

Days that had been filled with backbreaking, sweaty work as they'd started to empty out, clean, and organize the attic and second floor rooms. And despite the fact that they'd all—with the sometimes exception of Lena—wound up falling into bed exhausted from their efforts, thoughts of the note and who might be behind it had been plaguing her long after dark.

"These things often go unsolved," Kate said with a shrug. "Unless it happens again, I'm not holding out a lot of hope that we're going to find the culprit."

They'd already gotten the window fixed, and aside from the strange sense of unrest, it was almost like it had never happened.

Only, it had...

"Has anyone heard from Sheriff Fletcher?" Maggie asked,

shooting Lena a quick glance. Her oldest sister ticked a strand of silver hair behind one ear and shook her head.

"Not since he mentioned having a potential lead at the cafe the other day. I'm with Kate. I think the less oxygen we give it and the less we talk about it outside the house, the quicker the fire will burn out. People do that kind of thing to get a reaction. If we keep our heads down and do what we're here to do, whoever was behind it likely won't bother next time."

Maggie frowned but didn't argue as she stood and began gathering up the dessert plates.

"I know your mama wouldn't have called you all to come stay here if she thought you'd be in any kind of danger, but if anything like that happens again--"

"We'll call the Sheriff and keep you posted," Kate assured him, patting his hand gently. "Promise."

Sasha shot Kate a pointed glance, letting her sister know that she was taking note of that promise herself and wouldn't hesitate to call her on it if she had to.

"Before I forget, I have some things I think Maeve would want you girls to have," Harry said, getting out of his chair with some effort and hobbling out of the dining room, only to return a few moments later with a tattered, leather briefcase.

He set it on the table and popped the locks on either side before flipping it open. His face crumpled for a split second before he got a hold of himself as he pulled out a pile of pictures and a file folder.

He stared at the top photo for a good, long moment, and then set it in the middle of the table so all of them could see. It was an eight by ten black and white image of Maeve in her early thirties. She was wearing a one-piece maillot style bathing suit that flattered a figure that would've put Jayne Mansfield to shame. Flanking her on either side were the four of them, each in their own swimsuits. Lena was already old enough to be self-conscious, covering herself with crossed arms, but the rest of them were hamming it up for the camera. Sasha had one hand on her hip, flashing a gap-toothed smile. Maggie's head was tipped back in laughter, her diaper poking out over the top of her flower-dotted bikini. Even the always more reserved Kate was grinning from ear to ear.

If Sasha's memory served her, the shot had been taken in Uncle Harry's backyard shortly after her father, Vinnie, had left but before Clyde had come into their lives.

Those had been some good times.

Sasha studied her mother's perfect face, wishing she could reach out and lift those oversized tortoiseshell sunglasses Maeve was wearing and see what was behind them. Every day the four of them spent entrenched in her past, decades of memories piled in every corner, it became more and more apparent exactly how tough their mother had been and how hard she'd worked to put on a happy face for her daughters. It had taken Sasha a full day to get over the letters between Maeve and Ollie that Lena had shown them, only to walk in on Kate rocking on the floor in front of Maeve's bedroom dresser, silently sobbing as she clutched a tiny satin bag to her chest.

Once Sasha had managed to calm her down enough to pry it away, she'd almost wished she hadn't.

In it laid a curly lock of blond hair and a thimble-sized locket with a name scrawled across it.

Beau.

None of them had worked up the heart to open it, even now, two days later.

Sasha had dug through the papers scattered on the floor next to her sister, finding a hospital record, along with a pile of yellowing, handwritten notes of sympathy, some from people who were still alive and residing in La Pierre. Turned out, Maeve had given birth to a stillborn baby boy between the time Lena and Kate had come along, and none of them had ever known about it.

And they said people in a small town couldn't keep a secret...

Sasha focused in on the image before her again and touched a finger to her mother's trademark, mischievous smile.

"I always wished I looked more like her," she mused softly, not even realizing she'd said it out loud until Kate cocked her head, brow furrowed.

"Everyone says you favor her most," Kate reminded her.

"That's cuz I work at it." She looked up and jerked a thumb at Lena, who sat beside her. "She's the one who looks like Mama, for all she tries to hide it."

If Sasha had ever wondered if their older sister realized it or not, she wondered no more. Lena's graceful throat worked as she looked away, at something—or nothing, more likely—outside the newly fixed picture window.

"She really does," Maggie agreed. "If you dyed your hair red like Mama's color--"

"She does dye it," Sasha said, leaning back on her chair and staring at Lena, waiting for her to deny it. "Gray, isn't that right, big sister? Has for years. What did Mama used to call it? Hiding your light under a bushel? Doesn't matter, though. People who look a little harder can see it. The cheekbones, the bow of your top lip that I always have to draw in, those curves most women dream of..."

She was surprised to find that saying it out loud felt a little like letting the infection run out of a wound. An achy hurt, but one with a purpose.

"You should let me strip out the dye," Sasha said softly, realizing the slow burns of resentment she normally harbored toward Lena was at an all-time low. "I can barely remember what you look like with the red."

"Me either, and that's the way I like it," Lena said, her curt tone bringing an abrupt end to the conversation. She turned her attention toward their silent guest and managed a smile. "It has been really nice catching up with you, Harry, but I have some phone calls I need to make to the West Coast before business hours are over, so if you'll excuse me."

With that, she stood and left the room with the bearing of a queen. Something else she'd inherited from their mama.

"I should be off anyway," Harry said, pulling one last envelope from the briefcase and then closing it with a smile. "My eyes aren't what they used to be, and I'm a menace on the road after dark."

"Next time, let me pick you up," Sasha said, giving him a hug and a smacking kiss on the top of his bald head. "Then you can stay as long as you like without having to worry about that."

"It's a deal," he said, patting her cheek affectionately. "Maeve was right. You girls are the best. We'll all talk soon, then."

They all walked him to the foyer before he paused.

"Actually, give me one quick moment, I forgot to give something to Lena."

Sasha watched, along with Maggie and Kate, as he ambled toward the study and knocked lightly on the door.

It swung open and their quiet exchange was brief. Harry came back less than a minute later and donned the hat that sat on the table. "Love you all dearly," he said, taking a moment to glance at each of them in turn. Then, he headed out the door.

"How long were he and Annalise married when she finally passed?" Maggie asked as the three of them watched him walk out to his car.

"I recall Mama making a truly awful cake for their sixtieth wedding anniversary," Sasha said, trying to recall when that was. "Maybe three summers ago?"

"Imagine a man whose wife becomes wheelchair bound and near catatonic less than five years into a marriage and staying by her side for a lifetime?" Maggie said softly, shaking her head in wonder. "You know how many guys would've dumped her off somewhere in an institution or something back then?"

"He wouldn't even let anyone else care for her until the last few years when he couldn't lift her any longer," Sasha marveled. "And here I gotta hustle to get a man to buy me a drink half the time."

Kate waved as Harry backed out of the driveway and honked the horn. "I'm starting to think they don't make them like that anymore."

Maybe to some people, on the outside looking in, Harry seemed faithless. After all, there was little doubt he and Maeve had been lovers on and off for years. The two of them—if the letters they'd found were any indication—brought together, at first, by the crushing, shared loss of Ollie in Vietnam. But to Maeve's girls, even Lena, Harry had been a fixture in their lives for good reason. He was her champion. Her defender. Her North Star when she lost her way. He'd been their mother's best friend in the world. And Maeve had been the same to him. It wasn't often a person found someone like that and Sasha was too busy envying them to judge them for it.

What must that be like, to have that kind of stability...a person that felt like home? For all her lovers, and there had been many, she didn't know.

But, man, did she crave it.

And, suddenly, it hit her between the eyes like a two by four.

I want to keep the house.

MAGGIE

Maggie stepped into the air conditioned office with a sigh of relief. Women in Los Angeles might get dewy in the summer heat, but women in their 40s in Louisiana? Sweat.

A squat, old woman sat behind the reception desk clacking slowly at an ancient keyboard in a single-finger hunt-and-peck that had Maggie grinning to herself. Her mother had typed the same way, when she was forced to do it.

Maggie snagged a butterscotch candy from the dish in front of her and leaned her elbows on the counter.

"Hey, Eunice, I'm here to see Alistair. He should be expecting me," she said. The old woman didn't react so Maggie went up and tapped her bony shoulder, smiling as she glanced up at her with a start.

"Oh, sorry about that, Lena, dear," she said. "I keep my hearing aid turned low so I don't have to listen to those doggone cicadas. Now what was it you were saying?"

Maggie didn't bother correcting her. To Eunice, all four of them were Lena, and even Sasha answered to the catchall name. "I'm here to see Alistair, he called for me a short while ago."

"Oh, you can go on ahead if he's expecting you. He isn't with any clients right now," Eunice said, pointing down the short hallway to her right.

The building's old floorboards creaked as she made her way to the office. Sometimes La Pierre seemed stuck in the past. Maggie remembered the same creaking when Maeve had left her with Eunice while heading into Alistair's office to talk about God knows what. She smiled fondly as she remembered the old woman letting her eat way too much candy.

"Feel free to sit, Miss Maggie," Alistair said, rising in a quaint gentlemanly fashion until she sat. "How are you holding up?"

"As well as I could be, given the circumstances," she said. "How about yourself?" she added, tired of the question but trying not to be short with her mother's dear friend. It wasn't his fault her emotions were so close to the surface all the time lately.

"About the same. Still can't quite believe she's gone," he said, shaking his head with a sorrowful look on his face. "I guess I'll get straight to the point so you can get on with your day. Maeve wanted me to wait for things to settle in a bit before I started discussing business matters, but I think it's about time I gave this to you." He handed her an unsealed envelope with a small folded note inside.

Maggie took it out, unfolded it, and began to read...

To my youngest, Maggie,

CHRISTINE GAEL

Lately, I've had a lot of time on my hands and I've spent an embarrassing amount of it considering what kind of stamp I'm going to leave behind on La Pierre when I go. Surely I'll be punished for my vanity at the pearly gates, but I'm a woman of habit and I've grown to love my faults as much as my virtues. Once the last betrayed wife and scorned lover pass from this world, who will remember me but my children and Harry? And even those memories won't be as fond as I would've wished. I'm sure you know that, as I aged, my youthful passion for men and money began to fade and, at first, I thought I was happier for it. But I am nothing if not a greedy woman, and a new lust has taken their place; a lust to be remembered. For my life to have meant something. It is for the satisfaction of this prideful desire that I write this letter for you, my dear daughter.

To some, Lena, who was always the scholar and a natural leader, would be the obvious choice to ensure my name lives on. But it's you who shares my entrepreneurial spirit. I always found it funny that my sister Claire, always a free spirited artist rather than a capitalist by nature, birthed my only daughter with the same drive I'd been blessed with. For that reason, it took very little consideration to entrust you, Maggie, with the future of my enterprises. The business has declined as steadily as my health, of late. Last summer, as you know, I handed over the day to day running of The Luxe to Martin Bissett. He's a good man and would do well as a right-hand man, but he has no vision. Left to his own devices without direction, he will run it into the ground eventually. In addition, I want to continue my charitable giving and finally get my foundation out of the planning stages and off the ground. You can do that for me, Maggie. I know you can. I've left documents with Alistair detailing your position, in both the business, as well as the non-profit. If you choose to accept the position as outlined, profits from The Luxe, should it begin to run in the black again, will be split. Half will go to you for your efforts, while your sisters split the other half between them. If you choose not to run the business, you can sell it and the four of you will split the money evenly.

I've done my part to express my wishes as clearly as I know how. Now I'll leave you to figure out how to break it to the other three. I know you'll do a wonderful job if you choose to take on this responsibility, but know that, regardless, I love you dearly and I wish nothing but the best for you.

All My Love,

Mama

Maggie wiped a tear from her eye and set the letter down, still reeling as she looked up at Alistair. "I assume you already know what this is about, do you have the documents that she discussed?"

"Yes. I would just need you to sign in a few places, assuming you're not planning to sell," he said, pulling out three pieces of paper.

"I'm going to need to sit with this a few days and then discuss it with my sisters. Can I take those with me?" Maggie asked. This was a decision that all of them should make together.

"Certainly. But please know that your mama intended this decision to be yours and yours alone. No consensus needed," he said, glancing at her over the rim of his glasses.

She said her goodbyes to Alistair and made her way back into the main lobby of the ancient building. "Have a good afternoon,

Eunice," she shouted loud enough for the old woman to hear as she walked out of the building.

"You too, Lena, I'll see you around," she replied.

Maggie's mind raced as she walked home, but her legs definitely didn't. She needed some time to think as a million questions buzzed through her head. How was she going to tell her sisters about all this? What would they say about the business being in her control when she wasn't even Maeve's biological daughter? Would they want to sell?

The one thing she didn't have to question for a second was whether or not she wanted to step into Maeve's role, both in the business and in the non-profit. It was her mama's legacy. More than that? She had entrusted Maggie to honor it.

She wouldn't...couldn't let her down.

By the time Maggie was halfway through the long trek back to the house, she had made up her mind to pay Martin Bissett a visit and get some information about the casino before she mentioned her visit with Alistair, and what came of it, with her sisters. When they spoke, she wanted to be armed with information and data that would hopefully make all this easier to swallow. Because as much as she was shaken and moved to the core by Maeve's faith in her, the thought of it causing friction between she and her sisters made her gut clench.

She spent the rest of the walk home running through every possible scenario, thinking about Sasha and Lena's reactions to the news. Surely, as the oldest, Lena would feel that it should've been at least offered to her. And wouldn't Sasha be offended at being overlooked as the one who was closest to Maeve and spent the most time with her, especially these last few years?

When she was just a few blocks from the estate, she passed the Russell and Sons Confections Shop and impulsively veered off to head inside. The musty scent of the old building, mixed with the sweet smells of cooked sugar and cinnamon, wasn't at all unpleasant, though maybe that was more due to the nostalgia that came along with it than the odor itself. A young man no older than twenty stood behind the counter, smiling.

"What can I get for you?"

"I'll just take a pound of your toffees," Maggie said.

The boy took a metal scoop and dropped an overflowing portion of the wrapped candies into a tiny paper bag and handed it over to her.

"That'll be four dollars," he said, taking the five-dollar bill she held out to him.

"Thanks a lot," she said, unwrapping two of the toffees and tossing them into her mouth at once. The buttery taste instantly brought an image of her mother to her mind. Funny that she had once hated the stuff, thinking it a candy for old people and preferring chocolates or caramels. As she walked out the door, she wondered absently if Maeve had even liked the stuff before Ollie passed away or if she picked up a taste for them after he was gone, like Maggie seemed to have with her mother.

Her thoughts were interrupted as she saw a familiar-looking woman a few years older than herself walking down the street, coming from the opposite direction. The other woman waved and smiled, sweet as the candy Maggie was eating, but her instincts told her that she was no friend of hers.

Why couldn't she place her?

"Hello, Maggie. Long time, no see," she said in a two pack a day voice that resonated through Maggie like a sharp pinch.

Maggie waved, too many toffees in her mouth to speak through, and kept walking. It took another few minutes of brain wracking before Clyde's tired, rawboned face popped into her head, clear as a picture. Serina McFadden, Clyde's daughter.

She'd looked much the same when she was a girl as she did now, exactly like her daddy, only with longer hair and fuller lips.

A shiver ran through her as she tried to digest this new information. No doubt, Maeve's death had something to do with why she was back in La Pierre. By the time she opened the door to the house, she was quivering with anxiety.

"Who's here?" she called, closing the door behind her.

"Me and Kate are in the living room," Sasha called.

Maggie set down her purse and followed the sound of her voice. The two of them were cleaning out a bookshelf, by the looks of it, and dozens of journals and papers sat open, many of them handwritten in her mama's own script.

"Serina's back in town," Maggie said breathlessly, getting straight to the point.

"That little sneak," Sasha muttered, "probably thinks she's entitled to some inheritance or something. Over my dead body."

"Wouldn't put it past her to have something to do with that rock through the window the other day," Kate said, looking thoughtfully at Maggie.

"Do you know where she's staying? Maybe I need to go have a woman to woman talk with her," Sasha said, almost snarling as she said it.

"Slow your roll," Kate said, putting a hand out, "Lena is working on her paper for another half hour or so. We should wait for her to finish up and talk this out between the four of us. It'd be best if we don't escalate this any further than we have to."

Sasha looked at Kate angrily but nodded. "We can wait for Lena but I'm pretty sure she's going to agree with me."

"Is there any way she's just here because she wants to pay her respects?" Maggie asked hopefully.

"There sure isn't," Kate replied with a sigh. "If the McFaddens are sniffing around La Pierre, they're bringing trouble with them. Count on it."

All thoughts of her meeting with Alistair faded to the background as a sense of impending doom blossomed in her belly.

Dear God, please let her be wrong. This family was bending so hard, they were one false move away from breaking...maybe for good this time.

LENA

Lena stared at the blinking cursor in front of her, fingers hovering over the keyboard.

She had been prepping to send an email, but only the good Lord knew to whom about what.

Her brain was a sieve this past week. She hadn't expected to find herself so overwhelmed with dueling emotions. But so far, going through Maeve's house felt a little like grave digging. With every shovelful of dirt they lifted away, more bones were revealed.

Not that any of them had been fooling themselves before they started. They were all fully aware that Maeve had more than her fair share of skeletons. And still, knowing hadn't softened the blow with each new reveal.

Some had been emotional, but in a good way. They'd unearthed countless thank you letters from people in the community, from the baseball team she sponsored to the women's shelter in Shreveport she'd been a sponsor of since it had opened its doors in 1979. And the notes and cards from people in town she'd helped were just as plentiful, blessing her for loans she'd offered without being asked, or rides to and from the hospital.

Mixed in with those, though, was some less heartwarming correspondence. A handful of letters from furious wives, demanding she keep her legs closed or suggesting she leave town and move to Vegas where "women like her" were more welcome. Legal letters and documents outlining her brushes with the law. Maeve had never done any hard time, but she'd spent more than a night behind bars before Alistair managed to get her out, and she'd even been on house arrest for a time awaiting a racketeering trial. In the end, Maeve had prevailed. Seeing all of this stuff and learning about some of it for the first time ever, had brought all those memories she'd tried to forget rushing back to the forefront.

How many times had she been forced to miss school because Maeve was out all night on the riverboat and hadn't gotten back by morning in time to care for Sasha or Maggie? How many times had she stayed awake by the window, imagining her mother dead on the side of the road somewhere or bobbing, lifeless, in the lake because some desperate gambler didn't have the money to pay his debt, or a jealous wife had finally decided she'd had enough of Maeve Blanchard?

So very many.

Her email pinged with a new message and she squeezed the bridge of her nose between thumb and forefinger when she saw the name of the sender.

Trent Loughlin, her attorney.

She double-tapped and scanned the email quickly before reading it again carefully.

. . .

Sorry, Lena, I read this myself and then gave it to my partner for a second opinion. No matter how we turn it, this thing is airtight. Now, we can try to establish that your mother wasn't in her right mind when she signed, but it's a long shot. And, regardless, by the time we got a ruling, the three months would be long past. If you leave now, we'd be fighting against the beautification committee after the fact, with a relatively low expectation of winning. If you want your sisters to get their inheritance, staying is the only way to guarantee it. I'm sorry, I wish I had better news.

Trent

She'd expected the rush of disappointment. This had been her last hope of getting out of La Pierre and back to her old life anytime soon, after all. But nothing was simple or cut and dried when it came to Maeve, because she hadn't expected the strange sense of relief that had been mingled in with her disappointment at Trent's reply. Sure, she'd still have gone back home if it were a possibility, no question of that. The lure of the known and comfortable versus this daily riot of conflicting emotions was strong. But she would've left wondering if she should've stayed. There were a lot of loose ends here that she'd spent a lot of years trying to ignore.

Maybe it was time to start tying them off...Maybe, this time when she left La Pierre, she could walk away with a little less baggage, a little more clarity, and a clear conscience.

"Lena?"

She looked up to find Kate standing in the now open doorway, her face a strange mix of happiness and concern.

"I don't want to bother you while you're working, but the Sheriff is here."

"The Sheriff." Not, *"Joe".* Her sister's choice of words and the expression on her face led Lena to believe this was an official visit as opposed to a personal one.

Not good.

"Sure thing, I'll be right out."

"No need, I won't derail you from your work for long." Joe's long, lean frame filled the remaining space in the doorway and Lena's heart gave a jiggle.

"Oh, hi, Joe. Please, come on in!" As he entered the study with her sisters trailing behind, she forced herself not to glance down at the envelope directly in front of her out of some reflexive impulse. She was still grappling with her complex feelings about its contents, and had no intention of sharing it with her sisters *or* Joe.

Not now.

Not ever.

Joe took the seat across from her as Maggie and Sasha sat side by side on the couch, and Kate took the large leather chair next to Joe.

"So what's happening? Is this about the lead you mentioned the other day?" Lena asked, trying to act casual.

"It is," Joe said with a nod, dropping his hat onto his knee as he leaned in. "We have our man."

"Really?" Kate asked, frowning. "That's very interesting. Who was it?"

"Timothy Lischio."

Lena ran the name through her mental rolodex and came up empty. She was about to say so when Sasha sat up, bolt-straight.

"Tim? The kid who lives over on LaFayette Street with his meth-head girlfriend?"

Sheriff Joe shot her a quick nod. "One in the same."

Maggie gasped and Lena flicked a glance to Kate, who was also nodding her head, a grim smile on her face. "Makes sense."

"Okay, someone fill in the blanks. Who is Timothy Lischio?" Lena demanded.

Kate shifted in her chair and held Lena's gaze. "Serina McFadden's nephew. Clyde's grandson."

Lena tried her best to keep her face neutral, but her brain was on fire, churning up all the ramifications of this bombshell.

"We were actually waiting until you came out to tell you, but this fits in very neatly with what happened to Maggie just a little while ago," Kate added, turning toward Joe. "She was walking down Main Street and a woman said hello to her. It took a few minutes, but Maggie finally placed her face."

"Serina McFadden," Lena breathed, her pulse thumping so loud now, she wondered if the others could hear it. "She's in town?"

"She is," Joe confirmed, his firm mouth screwed into a frown. "For the first time in more than a decade. The question is, why?"

"Well, you said it was Tim, but what proof do you have that he's actually the one behind this? He never even knew his grandfather. Seems like if someone was holding a grudge about an old rumor, it would be Clyde's daughter, no?" Sasha said.

Lena thought back and remembered Serina as a wholly unpleasant little girl who stayed with them for a couple summers when Maeve and Clyde had first gotten married. She was a year or so younger than Kate, but she'd already had the disposition of a surly teenager. By the time summer was over, they couldn't wait for her to go back to her mother's in Missouri, and dreaded her return. If her constant whining and complaining was any indication, she was no happier to be there than they were to have her. The thought of her coming to La Pierre to rustle up trouble for them seemed in line with the Serina she'd known.

"He actually confessed," Joe said, scratching at the five o'clock shadow on his chin. "After I took a look around outside the other night, I saw some strange tracks on the outskirts of the property heading toward Butler Road. Footprints, but the left one was dragging, like. I remembered seeing Tim at Crawdad's not a week ago and he was limping. Said he fell off his dirt bike and pulled some ligaments. I took a chance, went by the house that night, and nobody was home. But when I finally caught him there a couple days later, I had a chance to talk to him and the girlfriend. She was twitchy as all get out. The second I started asking about that night, she was giving him looks. I made an observation about the dried mud on his shoes and that was that. He started squealing like a stuck pig. Took him down to lockup. He got bailed out this morning."

"Did he say why he did it?" Lena asked.

"He said he heard the story about Clyde getting killed in a mugging gone wrong when he was younger and his family never bought it. They just felt like Maeve's pockets were too deep and her influence in La Pierre was too great to overcome that they'd never get a fair trial. So they let it go. When he

83

heard about her death, he got riled up about it, and that was that."

"Sorry, I don't buy it. There's just no way he thought this up himself after all these years. Serina is behind it, I guarantee," Sasha said again, refusing to budge.

"When I heard she was the one who bailed him out, I made that connection, as well. Brought him back in along with his new public defender and he staunchly denied his aunt had anything to do with it. Swore up and down it was all his idea and she'd only come into town to get him out of jail and help handle the situation."

"You believe that, I've got a bridge to sell you," Sasha said with a sniff.

Lena cast her memory back and tried to recall the girl's relationship with her father. "Thing is, I don't recall her having any great affection for Clyde. I think it's possible that Maeve's death stirred up some old rumors and maybe got young Tim riled up. He probably had a few too many and decided to be a nuisance. End of story."

She didn't believe that at all, but the sooner they put this whole ugliness to bed, the sooner they could focus on what was important. Getting Maeve's affairs in order and making it through the next three months without killing one another. If Serina McFadden was after something, they'd know it soon enough. Lena would much rather have her come ask for it when the good Sheriff wasn't here for a visit, so they could deal with it quietly.

"When I spoke to Tim, he agreed to pay for the damages, so that's something."

"So long as he knows he's done wrong, that's good enough for me," Lena replied, shooting a quelling look to an already balking Sasha. To Lena's surprise, her younger sister stopped short of an outright protest, but she did stand.

"Okay, well, since the mystery is apparently solved, I'm going to go back to cleaning out the back bedroom. Joe, always a pleasure," she said, holding out a hand as if hoping he might kiss it. He gave it a firm shake instead, which had Lena biting back a chuckle.

"Good seeing you again, Sasha."

She frowned and then headed out of the room as Kate stood, as well. "I'm in the middle of something myself," Kate chimed in. Lena's cheeks heated when Kate sent Maggie a telling look that had their youngest sister following suit.

"Yeah, me too. I mean, I'm not in the middle of something, but I should be. See ya, Joe."

A moment later, Lena and Joe were alone. She debated pretending like that all hadn't just happened, and then thought better of it when she caught the flash of Joe's single dimple.

"Ugh, sorry about that," she muttered miserably as she swiped at some imaginary dust on the surface of the massive, walnut desk. "Kate has this notion that the two of us are some sort of star-crossed lovers with a history and a shot at a second chance or something. She reads a lot of romance novels. I hope she didn't make you uncomfortable."

"I'm completely comfortable, actually," Joe drawled as he leaned back in his seat and crossed his arms. "I'm looking at you, though, and you seem a little flustered. Feeling all right?"

If he hadn't been flirting with her the day they ran into him at

Beignet Parfait, he was definitely flirting with her now. Usually, her reserved expression and no-nonsense style kept most men firmly at arm's length. Then again, Joe Fletcher wasn't most men. Even when he was a boy, he was special. Kind. Strong, both mentally and physically. Mature beyond his years.

And a dang good kisser.

"I feel just fine," she answered finally.

"Good, I'm glad. I wouldn't want things to be awkward between us. Especially seeing as how I'd like to take you out for a meal tonight...catch up some."

Lena blinked, unsure of what to say. She was surprised to find she actually wanted to go. Surely, it was a bad idea, for a dozen different reasons, not the least of which was that he was the law and her mother had been the quintessential rebel. This house was brimming with proof of every shady dealing Maeve had been involved in over the past fifty-plus years, from old pink slips for cars she'd won in illegal craps games to ledgers from running moonshine. But that was all a long time ago. The Maeve of the past couple years had been tame enough. And, Lord, did she need a break from all the heaviness in the house. Every new secret they unearthed was like another shot to the heart. A meal with an old friend was just what the doctor ordered.

"Sure, I'd like that. What time?"

"I'm off at six, so how's seven thirty?"

They exchanged cell phone numbers and made plans to meet at a restaurant one town over. A couple minutes later, she walked him out and closed the door behind him, before she could change her mind. It was fine. They'd have some laughs and call it good. No big deal.

Besides, what had their mother always told them?

Keep your friends close, and local law enforcement closer.

She just had to make sure she didn't get *too* close, which would be no problem.

No problem at all...

SASHA

Sasha swiped a hand over her sweaty forehead and rolled back on her haunches. She'd started out just planning to clean the master bathroom but she'd had a lot of rage-y energy to work off and wound up making an executive decision to strip down the God-awful floral wallpaper. The Sheriff's visit had been doubly confounding, and between the news about Serina McFadden being back in town, and his upcoming date with Lena, she'd been fit to be tied. Not that she even wanted him, per se. But she wasn't used to men not wanting *her* and, for whatever reason, Sheriff Joe seemed entirely indifferent. The endless scraping and tearing was exhausting work, and had taken the edge off her anger, it had also wound up being a very worthwhile endeavor.

As she admired her handiwork, she had to admit, it was already looking a lot better. The massive, claw-foot tub was a showstopper and if she painted the walls china blue and picked up espresso-colored accent pieces, it would look like something out of Better Homes and Gardens.

Every day, this place felt more like a part of her. Granted, she'd spent a lot of time here at Blanchard Manor. Both when Maeve had first purchased it when Sasha was young, and for the past two years as her mother struggled with cancer. All that time, it had felt like Mama's house, full of Maeve's flashy style and influence. But now, as they peeled back the layers to the bones underneath, she was already feeling more at home here than she ever had at her own little house in Rawlings, one town over. Between that and memories they'd made here and the sense of history, she never wanted to leave.

How could she let it just get sold off to the highest bidder? Seemed like a crime. The problem was that her sisters all had an equal claim on the house and she didn't have nearly enough money to buy them out.

So what to do?

Kate had scheduled a walk-through with a realtor early next week so he could come appraise the house and suggest what other improvements needed doing before they put it on the market. If Sasha was going to make a move, it had to be soon.

"But first, I'm going to get me a glass of lemonade," she murmured to herself as she rolled to her feet. She washed her hands and then jogged down the stairs, ignoring the ache in her lower back. Like Mama had always said, hard work was good for the body and the soul.

Sasha slowed in front of the window overlooking the massive barn in the backyard, shaking her head sadly. It was really no wonder that families got torn to pieces so often with the death of a loved one. Sasha promised herself that she wouldn't let herself be the cause of that happening to theirs. If they didn't agree to try and figure a way to keep the house in the family, so be it. She would sell without fighting too hard, even if the thought of doing it made her sick. She didn't have much of a choice.

But she sure as shooting was going to ask. She just had to work up the courage.

She stared at the barn in the distance, already imagining what it could be. Surely, the distillation equipment would need to be updated. It had been years since Maeve had made any moonshine, even for herself. But Sasha knew deep in her bones that nothing would've made their mother happier than seeing her home be used to combine two of her favorite things; liquor and family.

Now if they could just get a poker game running, they'd be cooking with gas.

"What's up, Sash, just tired from cleaning all day or is something wrong?" Kate said from behind her. Despite Maggie being MIA for most of the morning and Lena working much of the day in the office, the sisters had made it a fairly productive afternoon. The place was really shaping up.

She headed into the kitchen and poured two ice-cold glasses of lemonade before bringing one into the living room for her sister. Kate accepted the glass with a smile.

"You done here for the day?" Sasha asked, gesturing to the bookshelves Kate had been cleaning.

"My brain says I can go awhile longer, but my shoulders are telling me otherwise. Why?"

"Come with me, I want to show you something," Sasha said, beckoning to Kate and walking out the back door. She took a long pull of the sweet-tart drink to buy time so she could psyche herself up. Then, she bit the bullet as she and Kate stepped into the balmy evening air. "I haven't told the others yet, because I'm embarrassed to admit it, but I quit my job. That's part of why I was so anxious when Lena walked out of Alistair's office. If we didn't inherit the house, there was no plan b for me."

"Why'd you quit?" Kate gasped, her steps slowing as they approached the barn.

"I hated working at that place anyways, so no big loss. The owner was a jerk and the clientele were a bunch of cheap skates. I have to be honest, I'm happy I did it," Sasha said, feeling her ears flush as she said the words.

"Sasha..." Kate said, trailing off briefly before continuing with a shrug. "You know what? I'm not going to lecture you. It was impulsive, but you're grown. And, honestly? I've always respected that about you. I've never been able to take that kind of a leap of faith, even if things aren't going well. But sometimes you just have to restart and hope the universe will guide you onto the right path. What are you planning to do once we're done here?"

"I didn't have a plan...at first. I just figured I'd work it out one way or the other. Worst case, I could live off the sale of my share of Mama's jewelry and such while we waited for the house to sell. But that was before we knew the content guidelines of Mama's will." She wet her lips and tucked a loose strand of hair behind one ear, forcing the words out in a rush. "I almost asked for my job back, but I stopped myself and I wasn't sure why. Yesterday it hit me, though. I was never meant to live outside La Pierre. Rawlings was fine, but this is where I'm happiest. So I had this idea..." Sasha said, gesturing to the barn twenty yards away. "Imagine what Mama would think if we kept the house and turned the estate into an actual bona fide distillery. Not a few moonshining stills and some mason jars, but barrels, moonshine, rye, the whole nine. She'd have loved that," she said breathlessly, eyes glued to her older sister's face, trying to gauge her kneejerk reaction.

"No doubt that Maeve would love it, but are you saying you don't think we should sell the house?" Kate said, looking around thoughtfully.

"I want it," Sasha said, feeling more comfortable because it was Kate. Reliable, gentle, non-judgmental Kate.

Kate paused for a long moment before saying, "We'd need to ask the other girls before we can make a decision like that. I, personally, don't mind it, though I'd like to get a piece of the distillery business if I'm to give up my share of the home."

"Of course," Sasha said, surprised that even Kate had taken it so easily. She really was asking a lot from her older sister. "You'd all get a piece of it and you could keep your quarter in case we ever decide to sell the house."

"Where would everything go? Would you sell the liquor directly out of the front of the house or would we find a distributor?"

"I was thinking that I could convert the garage into a little storefront for locals to buy, for starters. I think the barn is big enough for all the equipment we'd need and I have a little experience with the equipment from helping Mama when she was making it just for family and friends a few years back. I was thinking it'd be cool to make some of that peach moonshine like she used to bootleg back in the day, but this time with the proper permits and all, since liquor's legal in La Pierre now."

Kate studied her face. "You've really thought this all out, huh?"

"I have."

"I can't speak for the others, but I'm definitely willing to talk about some way to make this work for you. A distillery, huh?" Kate nodded slowly. "All right, let's try to think of a name for it, then."

Sasha sat for a moment, contemplating what to call it, then said, "Maybe we could call it, 'Maeve's Distillery' after Mama."

"I think we can get a bit more creative than that," Kate laughed. "Something like 'Miss Maeve's Marvelous Distillery'."

"Seems a little corny," Sasha said, chuckling. But she couldn't deny Kate's positive reaction had gone a long way to dispelling the last of the day's irritation. "What about something funny, like 'Maeve's Medicinals'?"

"Or how about 'Sweet Maeve's Distillery'?" a female voice called from behind them.

Sasha and Kate whipped around to find Maggie standing there with a wide smile.

"That's what Ollie called her in one of the letters we read the other day. Sweet Maeve."

"When did you get here?" Sasha asked, wondering how much she'd heard.

"A minute or two ago. You don't have to worry, I'm in. We just have to convince Lena."

"I love the name," Kate said. "Sweet Maeve's...What do you think, Sash?"

Sasha grinned, her eyes starting to sting a little. Dang allergies acting up again.

"It's perfect. It's decided. If we can get this thing off the ground, we'll call it Sweet Maeve's. Nothing would've made Mama happier."

"No reason to get any further into the details until we know that Lena will even get on board. Let's head back and see if we can ask her before the date," Kate said.

Sasha tried not to let the sour feeling in her gut show on her face when she thought of the Sheriff turning down her advances like she was some kind of child, only to go chasing after Lena. After all, it hardly mattered. But if Lena looked at her with that same expression? Like a grownup who was tired of humoring her?

She was liable to spontaneously combust.

"Actually, I'd rather not talk to her about it just yet. Let's wait till we have a bit more time to discuss it seriously."

"Sure, but don't wait too long. Once we sign with the realtor and start investing in major repairs, it's going to be a lot harder to untangle. Seriously, though, Sash. I'm in awe of you. Taking a risk like that and daring to dream big. Mama would've loved that more than anything," Kate said.

Sasha nodded and began moving back towards the house, Kate and Maggie following. "You know, Kate, you should really take the same kind of advice you give me and put it into action for yourself. Just saying," Sasha said, looking over her shoulder but continuing to walk. "You can take a risk and have some dreams of your own, you know..."

Kate looked up from her phone, no doubt reading a text from Frank, asking her for instructions on how to wipe his butt, and shot her a bittersweet smile that was equal parts longing and resignation. "If only it was that easy."

When they stepped back into the house a minute later, they

found Lena putting on a pair of heels, ready to head out the door. Sasha hated the jealousy bubbling up inside her, but the dislike of it didn't make it just go away. She stalked back to her room as Kate and Maggie wished Lena good luck on what would almost certainly be her first date in a long time.

She pulled the jar of Maeve's Peach Moonshine out of the cabinet under her desk and poured herself a shot, reminiscing about helping her aging mother make new batches of moonshine as she downed it. Fire burned a path to her belly as the taste of peach exploded on her tongue. Sweet, and intoxicating, but with a bite, just like Maeve. And just like with Maeve, if you weren't careful, you just might be kicking yourself in the morning when the spell wore off...

Sasha smiled as she admired the homey little jar. She'd probably had a hand in creating this very bottle, though there was no way to tell for sure. There were so many good memories for her in this house. How could she have forgotten that for so many years? She cursed herself for not moving back earlier, when Mama was still alive. Granted, she'd practically lived here once she'd gotten real sick, but had Sasha been here all the time before that, maybe she would've noticed something was wrong a little sooner.

A knot formed in her throat as she pushed those thoughts away. It was enough to put one foot in front of the other and get through the rest of these three months. When that was done, she'd give herself time to process. To remember. To regret.

For now, she had a job to do.

She downed another shot, turning her memory back to the house itself. It was like a literal representation of their lives. She remembered her mama coming home and announcing they'd be having an ice cream social that evening, so go on, run upstairs and put on your Sunday best. Or how she'd made even the most mundane task fun, dancing with a broom as she cleaned, and twirling them around the kitchen. Even when Maeve was gone, the sisters had each other. She thought of all the times she'd played tag in the backyard with Maggie and Kate, who always moved just slow enough to let her catch up. She smiled, thinking of Lena brushing their hair and braiding it when Mama was at work. And then there were the much darker times...all the men that Mama would bring around, Clyde being just one of several over the years. Maeve's swings from being high on life to short-term, but crippling, depression and back again. She had been a woman of extremes, both good and bad. The one thing nobody could dispute, though, was that she wasn't just alive. She was *living life*. And Sasha had spent her life trying to be just like her.

But that seemed like a wasted effort now that she was gone. Nobody could ever be like Maeve. She was an original, and it seemed silly to even try. Maybe now it was time to use the map and the lessons her mama had given her to forge her own path.

Sasha rose from the desk in the corner of her room, tossing back a third and final shot before heading downstairs toward Maeve's private study. Lena wanted it all to herself, but who was she to tell the rest of them what to do all the time? Lena had simply decided—as if she considered herself the matriarch of the family now...the new Maeve—that she got to keep the rest of them off the computer and out of the room. Being the only computer in the house, that hardly seemed fair. She booted it up and went on Facebook for the first time since she had gotten here.

The liquor had mellowed her some and she scrolled through her timeline, catching up with some of her friends on instant messenger. She'd been on for an hour or so when her stomach rumbled.

Time for some grub.

She logged into her much-neglected email before going to make herself a late dinner, and found a few dozen new messages waiting. Most of them were from one company trying to sell her something or another, but there was one from an email address she didn't recognize that had been sent the day before. The subject line had the hair on the back of her neck standing up.

Sometimes the past comes back to haunt us...

She clicked, but the email was blank, except for an attached image. With mounting apprehension, she opened the attachment and a large image appeared on the screen.

A picture of her mother stared back at her, only with red eyes and devil horns that looked like they had been put on in MS Paint. But it was the words beneath it that had her blood running cold...

LENA

"This is not a date," Lena muttered as she leaned forward to get a better look in the rearview mirror, pausing to tuck a stray tendril of hair back into place. "Not. A. Real. Date." Getting out of the car, she smoothed the silky fabric of her skirt. More than anything, she had to remember that she was here to make sure Joe—*Sheriff* Joe—would just let everything lie, at least as far as Serina McFadden was concerned.

Sure, her nephew admitted he'd thrown that dang rock, but that didn't necessarily implicate Serina. So long as Joe left it at that, Tim would get a slap on the wrist, and all this could all blow over. If he didn't and decided to push, or Serina stepped up this little game, at least Lena would have a direct line to what was happening behind the scenes. She'd squash it with Serina, and then everyone could simply move on with their lives. In a few months, Lena herself would be free and back in Seattle, where she belonged.

Alone.

With my studies, she tacked on mentally, countering the sudden, niggling doubts. *Happily* alone with her indigenous women's studies.

Not dressing up in silly skirts and wondering if some man she hadn't seen in years would notice she was wearing lip gloss.

She shook her head. No. She was not here for Joe's infectious smile, quick wit, or slow hands. She had a mission and she'd do well to remember it.

With one last deep breath, Lena headed inside the restaurant. She'd selected it specifically because the food was supposed to be excellent, but it was also located fifteen miles outside of town. She wasn't about to be seen out on a date at her age. Especially not by people in La Pierre. Maeve had handled their judgments with a wink and a smile and was as comfortable with the derision of her community as she was with the love they gave her.

But Lena wasn't Maeve.

The cool air washed over her as she stepped inside. A moment later, she spotted Joe already at a table in the corner of the tiny bistro. She slowed to a stop, instantly struck by his profile.

He had swapped his uniform for plainclothes. He'd looked great in his Sheriff's garb, but to see him in a button down shirt in a shade of blue that highlighted the extraordinary slate gray of his eyes. His collar, not quite buttoned all the way, revealed the column of his muscular neck and his dark hair, freed from its hat, gleamed with a hint of hair gel, neatly swept back from his rugged features.

Lena swallowed hard.

He certainly was a fine-looking man.

Just then, Joe turned and spotted her. His mouth tipped into a slow grin and he stood as she approached the table. When his gaze dropped to her mouth, she was transported back in time, a thousand years ago, when he'd pressed his lips to hers. She could still remember his sure grip on her waist as he'd pulled her to him. What she remembered most was how, when their lips broke apart, they'd laughed...nose to nose, breath mingling. It had been a long time coming, and the relief of all the anticipation had left them both giddy. But it only took a moment for the laughter to fade. Joe had let out a groan and pulled her close again, sending a pulse straight to her belly.

It was back, that thrum deep inside her, and it took everything she had to push it away.

"Joe," she murmured as she crossed the distance between them.

Focus.

"Lena." Joe's husky greeting set her heart pounding again. He pulled out a chair for her. "You look beautiful."

Lena flashed him a nervous smile and sat as he smoothly slid her chair into place.

Sitting across from her, he smiled again. "I'm glad you came."

Lena opened her mouth, but before she had a chance to say anything, their waiter arrived with a bottle of wine.

"I hope you don't mind?" Joe said as the waiter poured.

"Not at all." Lena took an exploratory sip of the crimson beverage. Crushed plums and black cherries rolled over her tongue with hints of black currant and spice. "Mmm," she said. "Delicious. I haven't had red wine since the last time I was back here."

"Why not?" asked Joe. He raised his glass and sipped, never taking his eyes off her.

She shrugged. "Seattle's more into beer than wine."

"If you'd rather have a beer, I'm sure--"

"No," she said quickly. "This is nice."

He grinned. "It is nice," he agreed. "I'm glad you suggested this place. I don't get out of La Pierre much."

Lena glanced around at the place and nodded. "I like the décor." Deep red, velvet drapes swathed the walls, strands of silvery beads hung from the ceiling, and jazz piano played softly in the background.

Lena blinked. "I think I've been here before, actually," she said before she realized it.

Joe grinned, nodded slowly. "Yup."

"Wasn't this... a Denny's when we were kids?" she asked.

"It was," he laughed, leaning in closer. "When kids would skip school, they'd come here to eat so no one in town would see them."

Lena couldn't help but notice the way his eyes crinkled at the edges.

"Well, I certainly never skipped school," Lena replied primly.

"You did once," he corrected. "A bunch of us did, and all went to the lake after..."

The memory came rushing back all at once. Splashing around in the water in the sunshine, feeling naughty as they sipped on strawberry wine, and then the bonfire that evening...

Her cheeks flamed and she cleared her throat. "I actually didn't remember this was the same place," she mumbled, resisting the urge to grab an ice cube and use it to cool her face.

"One of the best days ever," he murmured softly.

And now that she remembered it with technicolor clarity, she realized it had been. The perfect escape from real life. The one day she hadn't had to work five times harder than anyone in her class to get good grades because she missed so much school parenting her sisters. The one day she'd let herself be young and wild and free.

With Joe.

He lifted his wine glass and she followed suit.

"To Denny's." Lena clinked her glass on his and they drank their toast.

The next hour went by in a flash as they talked and reminisced. Lena had conveniently forgotten how much fun Joe could be— how he could make her laugh. Sort of how she'd conveniently forgotten all the good parts of the La Pierre she'd left behind. They sat talking about a thousand ridiculous things until well after their food came and they finally started nibbling at it, cold.

She enjoyed herself so much she didn't even pivot when the conversation turned to Maeve.

"I truly was shaken up when your mama passed," Joe was saying, his expression solemn. "I know you didn't always see eye to eye, but she was one of a kind. The town seems just a little less colorful without her in it."

She leaned forward on her elbows, meeting his gaze. "Maeve

Blanchard was a wildcat. Did you know that she got into a fistfight the first time she came to a PTA meeting?"

"I..." He covered his mouth, trying not to laugh as he shook his head. "I did not know that. But I'm not surprised."

"And did you know she used to run illegal poker games in the back room of the old ice cream parlor, over on Seventh." Lena let out a chuckle. "She'd have me sitting in front, eating ice cream while keeping watch as she ran games."

"Okay. That's something I never heard, either." He paused to take a bite of his steak.

"I loved my mother, but I left home for a reason, you know." Suddenly, it felt important for him to know that.

"I never doubted that. I may not have heard all the stories you're telling me, but I heard plenty of others. Seems to me, though, that you don't know what she'd been up to lately." There was no censure in his voice, but his words had Lena lifting her chin.

"We weren't exactly estranged. I spoke with her on occasion, and got updates through my sisters the rest of the time. Granted, we didn't discuss all her underground activities, but I imagine she was running some sort of fight club out of the women's rotary club," Lena said, trying to lighten the mood again.

Joe shook his head. "Hardly. Unless her fight club involves feeding and visiting with lonely senior citizens."

"What?" Lena had started to take a bite of her salad but froze at that, fork in midair.

"She started a Meals on Wheels type program, but local, up on the north side of town. Lena, the program she started feeds over two hundred people a year. She only stepped back when she got sick. Even then, she managed to write grant letters to every politician in Louisiana and secured funding to run it for the next five years." He took a bite of his surely ice-cold baked potato and then set his fork down. "She also started free daycare mornings over in the Palmetto Library," he went on. "And she ran a program over at the Farmer's Market every September where kids in need would get backpacks filled with school supplies."

Lena's chest felt tight and she pushed her plate away. "Maeve was a complicated woman, but you need to understand...she was no Mother Teresa. You didn't know her," Lena said.

"This isn't a judgment, Lena, but you haven't been around in a lot of years," Joe said, his eyes kind. "Have you ever considered that maybe you're the one who didn't know her anymore?"

Despite the careful delivery, his words stung and she drew back. Part of her wanted to lash out. Slap back, and tell him he was dead wrong.

But what if he wasn't.

"Dessert?" their waiter asked, breaking the tense silence that had fallen over them like a thick, oily smog.

Joe took the dessert menu their server extended and laid it down between them. "What do you say, Lena?"

Their waiter might think that question was about dessert, but Lena knew exactly what Joe was asking. Did she plan to stick in for a while, or was she going to run off now that things had gotten a little more complicated, and he'd called her on her BS.

"Maybe," she said finally as the waiter cleared their dinner plates. "Just one to split, though. I'd never be able to finish one on my own after that meal. Something sweet and salty," she said, leaving the decision in his hands.

"A salted caramel creole delight," Joe said to the waiter. "Two spoons."

To Lena's relief, their conversation seemed to flow easily again once the waiter left. When he returned not ten minutes later, the pressure in her chest had eased. He set a plate between them and Lena groaned. A cloud-like layer of whipped cream sat atop a thick, gooey layer of salted caramel, oozing down the sides of a fudgy, nut-studded brownie.

"What makes this heart attack in a dish creole?" she asked.

"The spice," Joe answered. "According to the menu, it's a cinnamon whipped cream and the brownie has a kick to it."

Lena picked up a spoon and said a prayer that her skirt buttons would hold as she dug in. As the airy puff dissolved on her tongue, creamy cold contrasted with still-warm chocolate, fudgy and yet still cakelike, to be followed with silky sweet sugar and salt.

Lena closed her eyes and all but shuddered.

"Well, that's a ringing endorsement if I ever saw one," Joe murmured, voice low and gritty.

Lena opened her eyes to find him staring at her like she was the only person in the room.

A low, persistent buzzing filled her ears and, at first, she thought it was just the blood rushing to her head. It took a second to make her realize it was her phone. Frowning, Lena bent over and scooped it up, but it had already gone to voicemail. With a murmured apology to Joe, she unlocked the device.

Two missed calls. Three texts. All from Sasha.

She and Joe must've been chattering away the other time her phone rang and she hadn't heard it. She dove into the text messages first.

No information there, just *Pick up,* and *Call me right now,* and *Answer your phone!*

"Useful," she muttered.

Her phone buzzed again with an alert to the unheard voice message.

Lena pressed a button and held the phone to her ear, holding one finger up to fend off the obvious questions from the other side of the table.

"Lena, thank God y— Oh. Voicemail. Nice. Fine. Just... just call back." Sasha's texts had been pretty standard, for Sasha. Pissed and huffy, sure, but that was par for the course with her little sister. What had Lena's hackles up was how frantic Sasha had been at the beginning of the message. But she couldn't very well call her back with Joe sitting across from her. Who knew what this was all about?

"Problem?"

"Actually, I've got to go," she said with a smile. "Seems like there is an issue with the pipes in the bathroom and my sisters can't get ahold of the handyman."

"Anything I can help with? I'm pretty handy myself."

Lena shook her head and reached for her bag. "I'm good with a wrench myself. We'll take care of it, but I appreciate the offer."

She couldn't help but notice the fleeting look of disappointment that crossed his handsome features.

"I'll get the check and walk you out, then."

A few minutes later, they were stepping out into the sultry night air. He walked her to her car in silence, only breaking it when they came to a stop beside the driver's door.

"Maybe we can try this another time?" At her hesitation, he pressed on. "Not the same place, of course." He smiled at her. "There's this great little theatre over on Thurmund. They serve you a three-course meal during the movie."

"I..." She evaded his gaze. If she looked into those bright eyes, she just knew she'd be lost. "I'm not sure, Joe. I don't think I can," she said, her voice sounding thin. "I had a great time, but there's so much going on right now." Maybe even more than she knew about, if Sasha's frantic call was any indication. This had been a bad idea from the start. She'd wanted to spend time with him, and had given herself an excuse to do it. But it all seemed so flimsy now.

"I understand," he said softly. "I guess I'd better do this now, then, in case it's another forty years before I get the chance again."

She was still trying to make sense of his words when he slipped his arms around her hips and pulled her close, slowly enough to give her a chance to pull away.

She didn't.

A second later, his warm lips brushed against hers, soft and sweet. She could smell the caramel and cream on his breath. For a heartbeat, she froze, uncertain. Then she melted into him. The kiss was everything she remembered. His scent hadn't really changed; his lips still felt gentle, yet eager. He wrapped his arms around hers, holding her close for another instant before pulling away.

"It was great spending time with you, Lena."

He turned to go, but before he'd taken a step, he turned back, his eyes blazing with something she couldn't name.

"Humans are creatures of habit, Lena. You ever think you've been running away from La Pierre for so long, you don't even know what you're running from anymore?"

He didn't wait for her reply as he crossed the parking lot in long, sure strides.

Yep, no question about it. Dinner with Joe Fletcher had been a bad idea.

One she was pretty sure would haunt her for days...and nights to come.

KATE

A murderer's got to pay one way or another. We'll be in touch.

Kate stared at the screen again, a ball of ice forming in her belly.

"This is going too far," she said, folding her arms over her stomach as she tried not to panic. "I can deal with gossip and the like, but the threats? Even after Sheriff Joe warned them?"

Maggie raked a hand through her cap of dark curls and pushed away from the desk. "You'd think they'd be at least a little nervous. It's not like they have a whole bunch of money to keep bailing Tim out of jail. And last I heard, Serina's husband left her and she was shacking up with some loser in a seedy part of Memphis. Whatever they think they have on Maeve must be pretty damning to feel so confident."

The front door slammed a second later, and Lena's voice rang down the hall. "Why isn't anybody picking up their damn phone?" She thundered into the room, scowling at Sasha, who was seated behind the desk. "This better not be some silly nonsense like that time you called me home from working at the ice cream shop, saying it was an emergency and me coming home to find out Maggie had used one of your crayons."

"I was, like, five years old," Sasha shot back, her tone pure venom. "You need to stop dwelling on the past. But you know what, forget I called. We've got it all under control. Why don't you go back to your date and the rest of us will take care of this like we do everything else around here?"

"She's just scared, Sash," Kate admonished quietly. "Sorry, Lena, we all came rushing in when the email came and I didn't think to grab my phone. We've just been in here ever since, trying to figure out how to handle it."

"Oh, see, you must be under the impression that I have any idea what you're talking about right now." Lena shook her head and laughed without even a hint of humor. "Your sister sent me three texts saying absolutely nothing, followed by a voicemail saying even less. Someone want to fill me in?"

"We got another threat. This time it came to Sasha via email." Kate straightened and stepped back to make room for her oldest sister.

The anger drained from Lena's face and she rounded the desk. Sasha leaned away from her as she scanned the short message.

Kate could almost hear her gears grinding as she tried to figure out their next best steps.

"Is your email address public, Sash?" Lena asked briskly, slipping seamlessly from anger into calm, collected crisis-mode.

"I don't know," Sasha shot back sullenly. "I don't have it plastered on my bumper or something, if that's what you mean."

"Do you list it on social media, like Linked Up or anything, or would only the people you've given it to have it?" she pressed.

"I probably put it on my Facebook when I first opened my account, yeah. And who the hell uses Linked Up?"

To her credit, Lena ignored the jab as she leaned in and forwarded the message to her own email address. "I'm sure the email address it was sent from is a one and done, but maybe there's another way to trace it. I need to talk to Alistair. Until I do, we say nothing of this to anyone. You understand?"

Maggie and Kate both nodded, but Sasha seethed. "I don't even know why I called you. There was a hundred percent chance you were going to come and try to take over the situation and boss us all around, like you always do." She pushed back the chair and stood. "I'm going to make myself a drink."

She stalked away, leaving the three of them staring behind her.

It had been a long few weeks for the three of them living in Louisiana, even before they'd all moved into the house. Maeve's health had taken a hard right turn and, just when it seemed like she was pulling out of it and might have another few months left in her, she up and died. As prepared as Kate had felt, nothing could truly have prepared her for how she felt when she'd gotten the call. Since then, it had been a non-stop rollercoaster that she would give her left arm to get off of. The threats were just adding one more layer to the shit sandwich they'd been served.

"It was very upsetting," Kate murmured. "She's--"

"I'm not interested in you Doctor Phil'ing me right now, Kate. I've got to think," Lena muttered, rubbing at her temples.

"Okay, well, I think it would be easier for us all to think if you two weren't at each other's throats all the time."

Lena forced out a sigh and nodded. "You're right. I'm sorry. I had myself all worked up on the ride home and had no clue what I was walking into. I shouldn't be taking it out on you." She turned her attention to Maggie. "Can you please not go off half-cocked and call the Sheriff's office right yet?"

Her tone was even and steady, with no hint of sarcasm, and Maggie nodded.

"I hadn't even considered it."

"Here's what I'm thinking," Lena said, flicking a gaze between Kate and Maggie. "Serina has something that makes Maeve look bad. It's not enough to take to the cops or she would've done that already. My guess is it's something circumstantial that could be viewed as either a motive or a threat. Maybe even something that might be cause for a civil suit against the estate, hence her coming back to La Pierre now, right after Maeve's death. It's likely something Maeve could've refuted when she was alive, or Serina would've come knocking with her hand out sooner. I'd like to keep what happened between us until I have a talk with Alistair about what the estate's potential liability in this is and get his counsel. The tone of the message is scary, but if they wanted to hurt us, they could've and would've. This is about money."

"You're sure about that?" Kate asked softly, studying her sister's expression.

"Sure as I can be," Lena replied with a curt nod. "Sure enough that I would risk us all staying in the house, myself included, while we figure it out. I truly don't think any of us are in physical danger."

"Okay. I'm with you, then," Kate said, cocking her head at Maggie. "You?"

Maggie nodded. "Okay. But can you try to talk with him in the next few days? I don't want this all hanging over our heads for the next week without having any direction."

"Now we just have to see what Sasha th--"

The sound of a door slamming cut Kate's words short.

"That can't be good," Lena muttered, rushing toward the door of the office, her pretty skirt fluttering as she moved.

Poor Lena. She'd been out with a handsome, funny, sweet man and it had been ruined by Blanchard family drama, like so many other things in her life. She wished she could take the burden away for even a little while.

Lena came rushing back into the room, her expression grim. "Sasha just peeled out of the driveway. Donuts to dollars she's heading over to Tim Lischio's house. We've got to go get her before she does something stupid."

Kate's heart pounded as she rushed behind Lena, Maggie hot on her tail, as they headed for the front door. Lena snatched her keys and her purse up and they were off. A few hundred yards in the distance, they could just make out the wink of Sasha's taillights.

"She's such a hothead," Lena muttered, pressing her foot harder on the gas. "Is there some point in the space time continuum where a person is so totally unpredictable that they round the bend again and become totally predictable?" she marveled under her breath.

"What does it say about us that we didn't think of it before she left?" Kate said with a short laugh.

Maggie was quiet in the back seat, and that was probably for the best. The less they talked right now, the better.

As if Maggie had heard her thoughts, she suddenly piped up.

"I know that Clyde was killed after being robbed, but Mama didn't like to talk about it much, and you know how the rumor mill gets everything mixed up, anyway. Did they ever have any leads on who did it?"

"It was a year or two after I'd moved out west, so I only know what Maeve told me after the fact," Lena said, expertly navigating the dark, windy roads as she followed the taillights in the distance. "Apparently, he'd gone on a bender and lost a lot of money that day on the horses. He pulled some sort of scam where he wrote one of his buddies a personal check, and his buddy wrote one to Clyde, so they could cash them and then use those funds to win their money back. Back in those days, nothing was online or all that, so it didn't matter that neither had the funds to cover them. Their plan failed, and buried them deeper in the hole. Clyde was afraid to come home and tell Maeve how much he'd lost, so he made one last bet on credit, saying he had a buddy in the stands with the rest of his cash. Naturally, he lost that, too, then tried to scoot out. There was never any proof, but word was that the bookie followed him on the way out, planning to rough him up some. Things took an ugly turn, a gun went off, and Clyde was found dead on the side of the road the next morning looking like he'd been robbed."

"And what was the reason people thought Maeve had something to do with it?"

"She was hotheaded, like Sasha. Quick to anger, quicker to act, back then, especially," Kate explained. "You were pretty small at the time, maybe five or so, and after Clyde's passing, Maeve reined it in a little. Before that, though, things were volatile. She'd sent him to the hospital once after hitting him on the head with a frying pan."

"Wow," Maggie said, letting out a low whistle. "I'm glad I was only around for the tail end of that, then. Sounds scary."

"Well, lucky for you, you still get to witness her mini-me in action," Lena chimed in as she took a left turn onto Tim Lischio's street.

They pulled up to a rickety shack a few houses down, just in time to see Sasha hotfooting it up the walkway, a crowbar in hand.

"Crap," Lena muttered, popping the car into park behind a rusty pickup truck and shoving open the door.

Kate struggled to do the same with shaking hands, watching in horror as Sasha took the steps up the porch in one stride and went for the front door.

"Oh my God. I hope no one is home or she's going to get herself shot," Maggie said, practically falling out of the car after Lena.

"Come on out, you evil witch!" Sasha screeched, smacking the crowbar against the door and denting the aluminum in the process. "You got something to say to me and my sisters, do it to our faces like a real woman."

Somewhere in the distance, a dog barked, and a second later, a light flickered on inside the house.

"Sasha, get back here, you idiot!" Lena hissed as she sprinted up the walkway. "What do you think this is going to prove?"

"It's going to prove that if Serina McFadden wants to mess with the bull, she's going to get the horns. Nobody threatens my family. Nobody. Now come on out, you spawn of Satan!" This time, she didn't just bang on the door. She wound up and took a full body swing at it, shattering the glass of the storm door in the process.

Kate's stomach dropped as she tried to think of what to do next. There was commotion in the house now, and she wondered what its occupants thought.

Lena didn't waste any time wondering, and she didn't bother trying to talk Sasha down again. Instead, she charged up the stairs, snatched the crowbar from her, and grabbed their younger sister's arm in a vice grip.

"Get your butt in the car, right now!" she hissed, half dragging Sasha back down the porch steps.

"Or you'll what?" Sasha demanded, trying to jerk away.

"Or else I'll leave, and this time, I won't come back," Lena said. Maybe it was her serious as a heart attack expression. Maybe it was the solemn delivery of her words. Whatever the case, Sasha believed her and stopped struggling.

Lena led Sasha back to her car and jabbed a finger at Kate. "You drive my car and take Maggie back with you. I'm going to make sure Mini-Maeve here gets home safe and hope that Tim and his auntie decide they don't want to involve the cops in this mess. See you at home."

The dog continued to bark and more lights came on in the house, but no one came to the door, not that Kate could blame them. Seemed beyond foolhardy to engage the crazy that was happening out here.

She would've preferred to take a pass on it herself, except she didn't have any choice.

Family was family.

She just hoped Lena and Sasha remembered that, preferably sooner than later. Because, at this rate?

One of them was going to wind up dead or in jail before their three months was up...

MAGGIE

The beep-beep-beeping woke Maggie out of a fitful sleep, and she reached over to shut off her alarm with a groan. It had been a long, hellish night, and despite sleeping super late, she felt no more rested than if she hadn't slept at all. Still, she had a big day ahead, and was anxious to get started.

She rolled out of bed and made quick, quiet work of getting ready for the day. It wasn't until she was skulking down the stairs that she realized she was creeping through the house like she was some sort of cat burglar in someone else's home.

She shook her head and began to walk more normally. It wasn't like she was *actually* hiding anything. She was doing what any normal person would do before diving head first into a new business venture that could result in a tricky situation between family members. But there was no denying her relief when she found the house empty, save for Lena, who was behind the closed door of the study, tapping away at the computer keyboard.

Maggie stepped outside, closing the door carefully behind her, and then made her way to her car. The late morning air was cool for a change and she took the long way to Crystal Lake, letting the breeze wash over her face through the open window as she drove. She wasn't in a hurry, and she needed time to think about all the stuff going on with her sisters, in any case.

Last night had been a mess. If it wasn't her life, she might have even thought it was funny, in a dark comedy type of way. Dragging a forty-something-year-old woman into her car, after she bashed in a neighbor's door, before it escalated into some modern-day Hatfield and McCoy-level stuff wasn't exactly the norm for her. After Sasha had told them about the email, every instinct had been blaring that they should call the cops again. Serina was surely involved in this harassment and the email had certainly crossed the line from mere suggestion to outright blackmail. But now that she had more than just the vague idea of protecting Maeve's legacy to consider, she'd thought better of it.

Tim's arrest had already made the La Pierre Gazette, albeit in just a single line citing vandalism that had been mixed in with a host of other petty crimes the townsfolk had committed that week. But in a place where stolen turkeys and bar room brawls were the norm, a blackmail charge would get a lot more notice.

Obviously, going over to confront Serina and breaking the door wasn't the best way to keep a low profile or de-escalate the situation, either. There had to be a better way, but if there was, Maggie hadn't thought of it yet. And, apparently, neither had her sisters...

To her knowledge, at least. Something told Maggie she was missing some integral pieces of the puzzle. Pieces she was going to pry out of them tonight, if she could manage it. Once they laid all their cards on the table, her included, they'd surely be able to figure out how to attack this thing head on and protect both Maeve's name and themselves.

She made a mental note to ask them all if they could spend the evening together. Not in separate rooms cleaning, or in their bedrooms watching television separately, like they had been most nights. But like sisters, putting back a bit of Mama's moonshine and playing games. Something that would help them let off a little steam and maybe bond in a way that Maggie was sure Maeve had intended.

She was still deep in thought when The Luxe came into view. She was a big vessel, one of the largest structures in all of La Pierre, and Maggie could see it near half a mile away. As she got closer, her heart sank when she saw the condition of the old boat. It hadn't seen a paint job in years and the "L" had fallen away, leaving the sign to read "The uxe" instead. Based on what she saw so far, she had a pretty good idea of what it would look like inside.

Sasha pulled up to the dock and parked her car, taking a quick glance round before getting out. There was a beat-up Pinto pulling in behind her and, for a moment, her heart skipped a beat. Before she could make out the identity of the driver in the distance, the car did a one-eighty and pulled out of the lot. Probably just missed their turn. Apparently, blackmail and vandalism made a body paranoid.

Sort of like sneaking around did, her subconscious chimed in helpfully.

She wasn't sneaking, she reminded herself. Or, she wouldn't be for long, at least. In fact, if she had her way, she'd be telling her sisters about this visit tonight.

She shoved the twinge of guilt aside and walked carefully over the ominously creaking bridge at the end of the dock that led to the boat. Likely yet another reason Martin wasn't getting people in the door. Despite her first impressions, she was excited to go inside for the first time in more than a decade.

It wasn't quite yet noon, so the lack of customers lining up to get inside was no surprise. She was struck by the lack of staff, though. No one had even greeted her upon entering and, aside from the janitor scrubbing the windows, the section that should've acted as a reception area was empty.

The janitor looked up and gave her a wave, which she returned as she passed through to the main deck. Instantly, the smell of smoke had her wrinkling her nose and she winced as she looked around. Aside from a cocktail waitress, a croupier filing her nails at the craps table, and a dealer who was running a game of blackjack for two players, it was a ghost town. If that kind of ratio could be applied to the whole casino, it must be hemorrhaging money just on maintenance and utilities. Her spirits were slightly raised by the five or so people at the bar with menus in hand and drinks at their elbows.

She walked up to the scarred bar, waving as the barkeep came over to take her order. "Hey, can I get a whiskey sour?"

"No problem," he said, making the drink while she studied the worn walls dotted with photos of famous people who had visited the casino. Many of them had Mama in them, as well, including one with Dolly Parton with her arm over her shoulder.

So cool.

"Here you go," the bartender said, placing a glass in front of her. She watched as he put the bottle of cheap, mass-produced whiskey away under the counter and made a mental note to discuss a potential partnership with Sasha if things worked out the way she hoped. Nothing would've made Mama happier than seeing the two of them team up to revive the casino and her old moonshining business. Maybe it was just a silly dream, but the pair of them putting their minds to something was a force to be reckoned with.

She sipped the drink, eager to see how the bartender did with it, and was disappointed. It was far too sweet and she could barely taste the whiskey. Maybe she could get Ruthie from over at Crawdad's to come work here. She was a great bartender who made a good, stiff drink, but she was also quick-witted, warm, and smart. She would be a great bar manager and Billy Rutledge, the owner of Crawdad's, was a notorious cheapskate. Maggie was pretty sure she'd be able to get Ruthie to come over if she dangled the right bait. Mama had always liked her.

Maggie gulped down as much of the sweet drink as she was able to, and called the bartender over, paying and leaving him a dollar for a tip. "I was wondering if you could tell me where Martin Bissett's office is, I'm actually here for a meeting with him at noon."

"His office is back that way," he said, leaning over the bar and pointing to Maggie's right. "Go down until you pass the bathrooms, then take a left."

She nodded and followed his instructions, passing a small restaurant area with ancient wooden tables that desperately needed a paint job. The decor in the restaurant was completely dated, just like the rest of the casino. Everything was painted in a mixture of avocado green, burnt sienna, and Mama's favorite deep magenta. Everything that didn't smell like cigarette smoke looked like it did. She found herself wishing that Maeve had taken over the casino in the 50s, because, at least then, Maggie could've gone with a kitschy retro vibe instead of starting with something that looked like an eighty-year-old alcoholic's depressing man-cave. At least it wouldn't be hard to make herself look like some kind of magician when it was time to fix the place up, she thought, trying to stay positive. Some decent paint, and some new furniture, the place would already look a hundred percent better.

On a whim, she decided to check the bathroom as she passed it before talking with Martin, but immediately regretted it when she stepped inside. She barely noticed the ugly green tile because of how dirty the whole thing was. One stall was flooded with water on the floor, and there was mold growing in between the cracks in the tiled walls. The sinks looked about as you'd expect from metal sitting for forty years in a boat on salt water. She turned on her heel, trying to compose herself before going into Martin's office. There was no need to blame him. Maeve had given the casino over to his care when it was already failing.

To the right of his door, there were two pictures with dates in the 1970s in the bottom corner, one of the bar she had passed a bit ago, and the other of the front gaming room that she went through when she entered. She tried and failed to find a single thing that had changed between the photos and her memory of the rooms, other than more peeled paint and an extra layer of dust.

Reaching his door, she rapped on it twice and walked right in. "Hello, I'm Maggie Blanchard. It's nice to meet you," she said, smiling at the heavyset balding man.

Martin stood and shot her a nervous smile, gesturing for her to sit. "Hello, Miss Blanchard, it's nice to meet you. You mentioned on the phone last night that you had some questions for me?" He held out a hand to her and she shook it before taking the seat in front of his desk.

"Yes, as I mentioned, my mother's attorney suggested I come check the place out as my sisters and I try to determine where to go from here as far as the future of The Luxe." Might as well get straight to the point. She gave him a reassuring smile to soften the blow. "I understand that profits have declined significantly over the years, is that right?"

"Yes, ma'am," he said, "the Casino was already going downhill with the passage of time, but we were left rudderless with your mother's unfortunate decline in health." He looked at Maggie sympathetically and added, "I'm so very sorry for your loss, by the way. Your mother was a wonderful woman."

"Thank you for your sympathy," Maggie said, not letting herself get distracted by sentiment. "What do you mean, rudderless? You've been here in her stead, no?" She felt guilty at the way he squirmed but she needed answers.

"I was set up to take over the operation of the boat in her absence, but I'd be lying if I said I was well-suited to the job. Our staff is good and I can get them to work hard for me, but I simply don't have the bigger picture vision to see what changes need to be made. And that's not to mention a lack of funds and the layoffs that we've had to do over the year with the decline in business."

"What do the books look like, speaking of funds? I'd also like to get an idea of how much staff we are working with at the moment."

"We were in the red two grand last month," he said, "and the last time we were in the black was January of last year."

Maggie shook her head. The situation here was even worse than she had thought. "Where is the money coming from?"

"Your mother was paying it out of pocket and she left some funds to keep the casino running in her will. But, unfortunately, we're set to use that up by this time next year if it continues this way. And that's if we don't make any changes at all. Renovations would cost even more."

"And about the staffing? How many people are on staff and how is morale? Are they getting paid on time and everything?"

"We have 24 staff members left, basically down to a skeleton crew for a casino this size. They're good people and they loved Maeve. Even though many of them are forced to do two people's worth of work, morale is better than you'd expect. Especially the behind the scenes people, who I used to be in charge of. We used to have Lisa for the more front-facing members of staff, like the dealers and such. And to answer your other question, yes, they're paid on time. To my knowledge, Maeve was never late with a check and I wouldn't be the one to change that," he said, still looking nervous.

"And what do you think the problems with the business are? What changes would you make if money wasn't an object?"

"I think the decor is kind of dated," he said after a short pause, speaking slowly, like he was being quizzed.

"Agreed." Maggie laughed. "What about the gross bathrooms? That rickety bridge on the way in? The missing L on the sign? Hell, even the uniform that the staff wear is dated."

The enormity of the project bore down on her as she spoke, but it only served to ignite her determination further. She suddenly thought of a new use for the money she had been saving for the past eight years to pay cash for a house.

"And that's all before we even start talking about the marketing issues. I haven't seen any signs whatsoever for the place downtown, or any billboards on the highway. I bet most people in the area, besides those that live right in La Pierre, don't even know this place exists anymore."

Martin took a long pause, gulping before he spoke. "I don't really know about all that, ma'am. I was never meant to be a high up boss-type like this. I'm more of a middle-management kind of guy. Now that Maeve's passed, God rest her soul, I'm not even sure who my new boss is going to be."

Maggie didn't even realize her decision had been made, without the input of her sisters, until she answered him.

"I am."

SASHA

Sasha stared up at the swirls in the ceiling, finally catching sight of the one that had always looked like a clown to her from this angle. Her bottom and the back of her thighs were pressed against the headboard, sticking straight up as she stretched out her lower back. Between all the wallpaper stripping, crowbar swinging and wrestling with Lena, her muscles were in full-on protest mode.

She threw an arm over her eyes and let out a groan.

What was she thinking?

"You weren't," she muttered out loud into the empty room. Confessing her wrongdoings to others was low-ish on her list of priorities in life. She was a big proponent of the "suck it up, buttercup" movement. If you wronged somebody, try to do better next time and keep it moving. Spending a whole lot of time or energy on regret was counterproductive. Besides, the people in her daily life didn't do a whole lot of apologizing, so why should she?

Today, though, she was pretty sure she was going to have to bite the bullet and let her sisters know that she was fully aware that she'd messed up.

So far, the ramifications of her actions had been mild. Sure, Lena had chewed her out the whole ride home from Tim Lischio's place, but she'd half expected to be woken up in the middle of the night by Sheriff Joe knocking at the door for all the wrong reasons. To this point, though, all was quiet on the western front. No cops, nothing new from Serina or her flying monkey, Tim, and her sisters had all seemed to disperse in the aftermath of last night's drama. Kate had taken the trip back to her house for the day to replenish Frank's supply of frozen meals and run some errands, Maggie was MIA and Lena had been locked in Maeve's study since morning. It had been a lot more togetherness than what each of them was accustomed to for the past thirty-plus years, and there was bound to be some growing pains as they all figured out how to navigate this new, albeit temporary, normal. Sasha suspected they all just needed a little time apart.

Also, you messed up.

Like, bad.

"Oh my God, all right already, shut up!" she muttered to herself.

The phone next to her buzzed and she peered down to find a text message.

You free tonight?

The text came from a guy she'd saved in her phone as "ball-boy Allan". He'd been wearing an Atlanta Braves cap the night they'd hooked up after a particularly difficult day caring for her mom. She'd gone to Crawdad's to clear her head and had wound up back at his place. Since then, he'd messaged her twice. She'd been very polite, so far, explaining that her mother passed away and she needed to be with family right now.

Her phone pinged again and an image popped up on the screen. For a quick second, she wasn't sure what she was looking at, but then it hit her.

"Oh, lord."

Apparently, two weeks was the appropriate amount of time to allow a person to grieve before sending them pictures of one's twig and berries.

She deleted his contact information from her phone and then blocked his number. She knew what she wasn't going to do tonight, but the thought of sitting in this house and waiting in breathless anticipation for the other shoe to drop with this whole Serina thing, while she and her sisters tiptoed around one another, wasn't exactly appealing, either.

"Hey, you."

Sasha tipped her head backward to find Maggie standing over her, grinning down at her.

"Wanna get drunk with me tonight?"

Sasha swung her legs gingerly off the side of the bed and rolled into a sitting position with a grin.

"Absofrickinglutely."

Maggie held up a half bottle of Maeve's moonshine and shook it. "We can start with this, plus, there're two bottles of Prosecco in the fridge. That should do it."

Sasha snorted and padded over to her dresser. "And if it doesn't,

I got it covered." She held up her own mason jar of moonshine and grinned.

Maggie led the way out of the bedroom, and Sasha followed behind, amazed at how quickly her mood had shifted. The two of them had been closer over the years than either had been with Kate and Lena. Largely because they were much closer in age and had spent years with just the two of them in the house with Maeve, long after Clyde died and Lena and Kate had moved out. But also because Kate had been busy getting her nursing degree and then raising kids while Lena had avoided La Pierre whenever possible once she'd left. The past five years or so, Kate had been more present, making the drive at least once a month, but Sasha and Maggie stayed in close contact the whole time. No matter how busy her younger sister got with her freelance business or life in general, she always made time for their twice a week gabfest and their monthly meet up for drinks, just the two of them. It was weird how they were so different, but got along so well. Of course, raised as sisters, they still fought sometimes. But nothing ever got between them for long. Knowing that, at least, Maggie wasn't angry with her thawed the block of ice in her chest just a little.

It was wonderful having someone in her life she never had to pretend with and could tell anything to.

Well, almost anything...

"I had a feeling at least you were going to say yes, so I picked up a pizza from Addaro's and a box of cupcakes from Honeypie's."

"Sausage and fennel?" Sasha demanded, her mouth already watering. She realized with a start she hadn't eaten all day, besides a piece of toast with her coffee early that morning.

"Of course." Maggie began giving her the rundown of cupcake

flavors but, by then, Sasha's attention had turned backward to the rest of Maggie's previous sentence. She held up a hand and slowed to a stop. "Wait, what do you mean 'at least' I was going to say yes?"

Maggie turned slowly, one hand on the bannister of the spiral staircase. "Well, Kate is on her way back from her house now, and aside from last night with Joe, Lena's usually home, so I thought it could be the four of us. Together."

Sasha scratched at her chin as she contemplated the thought. She didn't want to let Maggie down, but the thought of being forced to sit in a room under the heat of Lena's disapproving glare for hours on end wasn't exactly what she'd been envisioning.

Maggie's pocket buzzed and she dug in and pulled out her phone, shooting Sasha a sheepish grin.

"Good news! Kate just pulled into the driveway and Lena is done working...They're both in."

Well, dang.

For a brief moment, the instinct to rush headlong back into her bedroom and drink alone nearly won out. It was only that deep, throbbing sense of guilt that had her legs propelling her toward the stairs once again.

She'd go down there, apologize like a grown-up, and eat dinner with her sisters. If it wasn't going well, she'd hightail it back upstairs to hide.

No problem.

By the time she and Maggie headed into the kitchen, Kate was already there, setting her purse on the table.

She wheeled around and shot them both a weary smile, until her gaze locked on to the jar in Maggie's hand. "You're an angel. I don't even need a glass. Hand it over, it's been that kind of day."

Maggie padded over and handed Kate the moonshine.

"That smell is killing me," Lena announced as she stepped into the room, sniffing the air appreciatively.

Sasha swallowed hard and turned to study the refrigerator magnets. Some of the ones shaped like the letters in the alphabet were arranged the same as Maeve had set them up before she went to be with the Lord:

Buck housework.

Preach, Mama. Preach.

Eyes pinned in place, she forced out the words that had been locked in her throat. "I'm sorry."

The sound of a jar opening and the patter of footsteps went silent as she chewed on her lower lip and pressed on. "Um, I know what I did last night was real stupid and I could've been hurt or gotten one of y'all hurt. That wasn't my intention, and I apologize, okay?"

Probably, she should've stopped at "I apologize", and left off the sort of aggressive-sounding, "okay?" at the end there, but hey...She never claimed to be perfect.

"Maggie's text said tonight was going to be our fresh start. A clean slate," Lena said slowly. "Far as I'm concerned, that's what this is. Serina or Tim or whoever is really behind all this will have a lot harder time messing up our lives if we stick together as a unit."

132

Strange. Maggie's invite to her had been an offer to get drunk and eat pizza. Apparently, the little scamp had tailored her invitations to accommodate each of them.

Smart.

Sasha pivoted and reached into the cabinet high above her head to pull down four glasses. Technically, they were for sherry, but she'd always loved them. Their mother had received them as a gift from a local glassblower who had made them especially for Maeve. They were three inches high and made of paper thin, magenta glass. The stems gleamed like gems under the pendant light as she set them on the kitchen island.

With little fanfare, she filled each to the brim with peach moonshine, and then picked up her glass.

"To cleaning the slate," she said with a nod.

Her sisters all joined her and held their glasses aloft.

"To cleaning the slate."

They tossed back their shots and then set the glasses down.

"Now, what say we get something on our stomachs so we can get serious about our drinking, ladies?" she asked, giving each of them a grin.

"Sounds like a plan to me," Kate agreed as the others nodded.

As they bustled around the kitchen in a seemingly choreographed dance of plate-getting, cheese grating, and slice serving, Sasha realized with a start that this was the happiest she'd been since Mama had died.

If only it could last awhile, for once...

MAGGIE

"So you're telling me that you're the one who broke my Walkman?" Kate demanded with a gasp as Sasha let out a peal of laughter. "You know I stopped talking to April Thorpe for a month after that because you told me you saw her sit on it at my sleepover party."

"I was a little jerk when I was a kid, what can I say?" Sasha admitted with a shrug, her face filled with impish glee.

"Sorry, maybe?" Kate shot back in faux indignation.

"If anyone is owed an apology, it's April Thorpe, but seeing as how I've reached my apology quota for this millennium, and April is now married to a banker, has a mansion in the Garden District, and drives an Aston Martin, neither one of you should hold your breath."

Maggie closed one eye and then the other, sizing up her vision. Yup. She could still see straight. Which meant they were all due for another shot.

"Glasses up, girls," she chirped, dragging the moonshine jar off the table and pouring as her sisters leaned in.

They all sat around their gently used but new-to-them coffee table, sprawled on the floor among pizza boxes and cupcake wrappers. The grandfather clock against the wall had struck nine and they were all deep in their cups, but the mood in the room was warm and easy. A far cry from the near-constant tension between them since the reading of the will.

Maggie let out a snick of disapproval as she poured the last few drops of moonshine into Lena's glass.

"Okay, looks like me and Kate are gonna have to take one for the team and settle for the Prosecco, because we are officially out of Mama's moonshine."

"Sweet Maeve's Moonshine," Kate corrected with a chuckle. "Remember?"

Maggie tensed and shot a glance at Sasha. "Um, yup, I remember..."

"What are you two talking about?" Lena asked, scooping up her glass and letting out a hiccup that sent them all into another laughing fit. When the chuckles stopped, Sasha clinked her glass to Lena's, knocked back her shot, and rolled to her feet, weaving a little as she did.

"Okay, on that note, since tonight is officially slate-clearing day, I have a confession to make."

Maggie ceased her efforts to uncork the Prosecco and gave her sister her undivided attention.

"I've been thinking and...I want to keep the house."

She said it like she'd dropped a bomb into a crowd, but since

Maggie and Kate both already knew, all their attention was on Lena as Sasha continued.

"I spent a lot of my childhood and a large part of my adulthood in this house. More than that, though, this was Mama's house. I feel her everywhere here. I just can't imagine selling it to some strangers off the street."

Maggie held her breath on Sasha's behalf as she eyed a silent Lena, waiting for the verdict.

Lena cocked her head and studied Sasha for a long moment, and then nodded thoughtfully. "Okay, keep talking."

Sasha wet her lips nervously. "Well, I was thinking, we still have the barn back there and all the equipment. Mama made a great product, everyone in the whole parish loved it. I'd like to get the permits, upgrade the equipment, and make it a real business. Hopefully one that can start to generate enough money to maintain the house."

"How are you going to do all that with your shifts at the diner and going back and forth?"

"I quit my job already. Don't get mad," Sasha said in a rush. "I wasn't being as impulsive as it seems like. My boss was giving me trouble about taking so much time off for Mama, and I was working doubles just to make ends meet. Whether this idea panned out or not, I knew I needed to find something else anyway."

Lena settled back to lean against the couch. "Makes sense to me. So what would happen to the equity? I don't need the money, but I'm sure Maggie and Kate could use it."

Sasha blinked and glanced around the room at Maggie and Kate, clearly at a loss. She certainly hadn't imagined Lena would be so open to this discussion. It was one thing for her to walk away from her stake in the house like she'd tried to do at the reading of the will. It was an entirely other kettle of fish for her to entertain an idea that both required her to stay and fulfill the three-month requirement, and still not walk away with a quarter of the house. Not to mention that it had likely seemed to come out of left field and was coming from Sasha.

"I totally get that. And if you guys would consider maybe pushing back the sale on the house by, like, six months, just to give me a chance to see what I can do, maybe I can figure a way to buy y'all out by then or, at least, start paying in installments." The excitement in her wide, blue eyes dimmed as she lifted her glass toward Maggie and jerked her chin toward the bottle, which jarred Maggie back into cork-prying action. "I know it's a huge ask of all of you. You don't need to decide right now. If you could just think it over, I'd really appreciate it, is all."

Maggie thumbed furiously at the cork until finally it leapt out of the bottle with a sucking pop, breaking the silence. She poured the golden, bubbly liquid into Sasha's tiny glass, and then her own, before setting the bottle down again.

"It's definitely something to consider," Lena said, shooting a glance toward Kate, who nodded. "I know The Luxe wasn't doing well the last time I'd heard, but who knows? Maybe it's been doing better and we can liquidate there some to make it work."

"After you left the will reading, Alistair told us he would get in contact about Maeve's business ventures early next week," Kate said.

Maggie had been waiting on the sidelines like a little girl looking for her window playing double-dutch, and here it was.

Time to jump in...

"I have something to say that might help influence this discussion somewhat," she said, downing a portion of liquid courage before she stood up beside Sasha. "Following our theme of full disclosure, I received a call from Alistair the day before yesterday." She paused, realizing that it was much easier cheering Sasha on than being in the spotlight as her older sisters eyed her expectantly. Despite the air conditioning on full blast to accommodate a house fairly brimming with menopause, sweat beaded on her upper lip. "I went in to speak with him yesterday and he gave me a letter from Maeve. It seems as if..."

How could she say it? How would they take it?

"It seems as if Maeve wanted me to take over the running of The Luxe and some other ventures, in order to secure her legacy in La Pierre."

If Sasha's news had landed with a squeak instead of a kaboom, Maggie's had certainly ratcheted things up a notch.

Kate's eyebrows shot high and Sasha rocked back on her heels as Lena stared at her, nonplussed, as if waiting for the words to sink in.

Not good.

"Look," she said in a pleading rush, "I know I'm not Maeve's daughter, and I'm not really one of you, and this probably doesn't seem fair—hell, maybe it isn't—but I really want this. I really, really want this. Maeve's brand can be a huge selling point if she had someone who knew what they were doing. I can make this work for all of us. Already, I went over to The Luxe and I can see exactly what--"

"Don't ever say that again," Lena hissed, her previously bleary eyes now as bright as chipped diamonds, and clear as glass.

"Wh-what do you mean?" Maggie asked, her stomach roiling. She didn't know which thing it was that had stoked Lena's fury, but it must've been a doozy. She swayed on her feet, breathless as she waited for Lena's reply. She wanted this, but not at the expense of her relationship with her sisters.

Lena scooted to her feet to join Maggie and Sasha, and closed the distance between them. "Don't ever say you're not Maeve's real daughter," she said, those green eyes still glittering. "You are one of us, Maggie. You always have been. What you need to do is stop selling yourself and your position in this family short. If anyone shouldn't be here, it's me. I'm the one who walked away while you all took care of Maeve through the hard times. So if we can stop passing around the chalice of guilt, maybe we can focus on figuring out how to do better for each other going forward?"

Maggie's throat went thick with tears as Lena dragged her in for a tight hug. Maggie was hugging her back as more arms embraced her.

"It's a sister sandwich!" Sasha exclaimed as they all rocked together slowly, laughing watery laughs. They stayed like that for a while before Lena pulled away with a shuddery sigh.

"I can't speak for Kate, but I'm happy to talk to Alistair and figure out how to make all this work."

"I'm speaking for myself, and I'm in," Kate said, pausing to snag a piece of cold pizza. "I'm in like Flynn. Whatever you guys want to do, we'll make it work."

"What about Frank?" Sasha asked.

"Screw Frank. He can decide what he wants to do with his part of his inheritance when his mother dies, although we all know that's never gonna happen." She tore a chunk of pizza off with her teeth and continued talking around it. "And even if it does, how much can a person really do with twelve cockatoos and two cartons of Pall-Malls, anyway?"

She snort-laughed at her own joke that got the rest of them laughing again. By the time they stopped, Maggie was breathless.

"I love you guys. All three of you. And, Sasha, if you want to talk business and how we can maybe work Sweet Maeve's in with The Luxe or work out a way to create a brand for Maeve that folds in both, I'd love to do that...when we're sober."

"Sounds like a plan," Sasha said, nodding as she leaned in and filched a bite of Kate's pizza slice.

"Seems like we're all set then. I'll talk to Alistair and find out our options. Until then, cupcake, anyone?" Lena asked, holding up the half empty box.

"I want a cupcake, but I also think we need to keep this whole full disclosure thing going, because I have a lot of questions for my big sisters," Sasha said as she plucked a coconut cream cupcake from the box. "Lena...did you or did you not let sexy Sheriff Joe get a bit of the old lady biscuit?"

Maggie squealed and collapsed back to the floor, laughing.

"I did not," Lena said primly. "And watch whose lady biscuit you call old, you whippersnapper," she shot back with a grin.

"Well, you should," Sasha shot back with a wink. "He's got those big, strong hands...I'm just saying, I think you're missing out."

Lena stayed quiet, but to Maggie's relief, she was still smiling as Sasha turned her attention toward Kate. "And what about you? Frank's like a sack of potatoes. You got a man on the side to keep that engine running, or what?"

Kate popped the last of her pizza crust into her mouth and shook her head. "Nope. But he really made me mad today, so if he keeps it up, I just might."

"What happened?" Lena asked, taking a seat on the couch and folding her legs beneath her bottom as she settled in.

"He was just a jerk. He didn't even get up when I walked in the door. Then all the complaining about the food I was making." She blew out a sigh and shrugged. "I'm just tired of it."

"Get up, then," Sasha said, the fire in her eyes igniting again.

"What do you mean?" Kate asked, brow wrinkling in confusing.

"What did Mama always say?" Sasha demanded, crossing her arms as she looked at them expectantly.

"Vows are fleeting but diamonds are forever?" Maggie said.

"Don't send a man to do a woman's job?" Lena chimed in.

"If you don't use buttermilk, it ain't fried chicken?" Kate asked, still clearly puzzled.

"Actually, those are all really good, too," Sasha conceded with a sage nod, "but I was going to go with, 'If you lay down, expect to get walked on'." She paused and held their sister's gaze. "So get up, Kate."

The grins faded as they all turned toward Kate.

"Ouch," she said, wincing. "But I know you're right, Sash. God, even when I went there today, he was such a jerk. No, 'how are you holding up?' or 'what can I do to help?' It was just, 'The meatloaf was dry, so I'll take more of the casserole instead'." Kate's bubbling laughter was more of an expression of disbelief than humor. "How did I get here?" she asked, tossing her hands up. "I know it's not all him. I've let him do this without penalty for years. But I don't want this life anymore, and I don't know how to fix it."

"What about counseling?" Lena asked gently.

"I would. I doubt he would agree, though."

"Maybe he just needs a wakeup call," Maggie suggested. "If you tell him you're not happy, maybe it will make him see things need to change."

Judging by Kate's dubious expression, it seemed unlikely, but the thought of her sister spending the rest of her years on this earth in a miserable marriage made Maggie deeply, deeply sad.

"It's all just coming to a head now with Maeve gone," Kate admitted as she lowered herself onto an armchair with a sigh. "I appreciate you guys having my back, but we have two kids and a life...I just need to consider this all really carefully and not be too hasty. It's been an emotional time and there've been a lot of changes lately. I don't want to do something I'll regret."

They all went quiet, sipping their drinks, lost in their own thoughts for a long while, until the grandfather clock chimed again.

"I have something else that needs saying."

Sasha's low admission jarred Maggie out of her almost hypnotic state and she turned to see that her sister's face was a bone-white mask of determination.

"This Serina stuff has made me realize we gotta stop with the secrets. So let's put it all on the table, all right?"

Kate's eyes went wide and Lena sat up straight, shaking her head, "Sash, you don't have to--"

"I need to say it out loud because it's like a poison inside of me and I need to get it out."

Maggie's head hummed as the words seemed to come at her in slow motion.

"I'm pretty sure we all know what really happened to Clyde, and it's time that all *four* of us know why," Sasha murmured.

Please don't let it be what she was thinking. Let it be *anything* else...

But as she looked deep into Sasha's eyes, Maggie knew her prayers would be left unanswered.

"He molested me, and Mama killed him for it."

MAEVE

November 4th, 1982

Dear Diary,

I'd always suspected it, but I was never sure. Today, it's confirmed: I'm a terrible mother. Far worse than even my own mother was.

My hands are shaking as I write this, because I've committed a betrayal far too deep to ever truly right, and my children have paid the price.

Especially my Sasha.

Three weeks ago, Marcus Battle made me a lucrative offer and I agreed to take he and some of his rich friends out on The Luxe for four days of gambling, drinking, and women. I'd had her moored for years, but she was still seaworthy. It seemed foolhardy to turn down the chance to have half a dozen millionaires in closed quarters with my casino at arm's length. Clyde agreed we could use the money, and never had an issue watching the girls if I had to be away overnight in the past. He wasn't a big talker, but he'd always cook fun things for them, like mini grilled cheeses with ketchup smiles, and franks and beans, only he'd cut the hot dog in a way that made it look like an octopus with eight legs. Believe it or not, it's one of the reasons I finally agreed to marry him. But leaving my children alone with that man was one of the worst decisions I've ever made, second only to marrying him in the first place.

I arrived home four days ago and, despite it being the most profitable four days of my life, I'd give my eyes to go back in time and change it. I was eager to see the kids when I pulled into the driveway, and couldn't wait to tell them about the plans I'd made for the whole family to go to the carnival over in Larrington the following day. When I walked in the house, Clyde was watching Happy Days on the television. He greeted me like nothing new, but Kate, Sasha and Maggie were nowhere to be found. I called for them and got no answer. It took me awhile to find them holed up in Kate's room.

The three of them were lying in Kate's bed when I walked in. She had Maggie under one arm and Sasha under the other as she read to them. I was a little disappointed...usually the girls would've jumped up to see me, only this time, just Maggie rolled off the bed to give me a hug.

I squeezed her tight, trying not to let my feelings be hurt, when I noticed how pale Sasha looked. I sat on the side of the bed and pressed my lips to her forehead, checking for a fever, and she flinched.

She flinched.

I turned to Kate, not knowing what I know now for sure, but my gut knowing it all the same, and I asked what was wrong. I hoped maybe Sasha was still mad about me going away for so long.

If only it was something as little as that.

Maybe because the truth was just too awful to bear, to my everlasting shame, I let it go and didn't press. Until yesterday. Clyde came into the living room while Maggie and Sasha were watching Saturday morning cartoons together. Kate handed him the remote and herded the girls into her room the second he sat down. I acted like everything was normal until he went to the store for a pack of cigarettes an hour later. The second he was out the door, I cornered Kate in her room and asked her again what was wrong. She didn't reply, and refused to look at me. I asked her if Clyde had done something to hurt her feelings. And, for the rest of my days, I will never forget Sasha's face as we both looked her way.

Her eyes were wide and her mouth seemed glued shut. I knew that face, though. I'd seen it in the faces of countless women. I'd seen it in the mirror. And that face told me everything I need to know.

All this to say?

I don't know how yet, but I'm going to kill the bastard.

KATE

Kate's head had a heartbeat as she leaned it against the cool stainless steel of the refrigerator door.

It was well past noon and this hangover still had legs. "That's what happens if you drink like you're in college thirty years too late." She let out a groan as she opened the fridge and peered inside. She'd stuck to dry toast, so far, but everyone knew cold pizza was the cure after a night of drinking.

"Grab me a piece, too," Lena murmured as she padded into the room.

Kate snagged two slices from the box and made her way gingerly over to the kitchen island and handed Lena her pizza.

"How you feeling?" she asked Lena as she took a seat on one of the high-backed stools.

"Emotionally or physically?"

"Either." Kate shrugged and blew out a sigh. "Both."

"I've been better. I'm making an appointment to talk to Alistair, to find out what we can do to accommodate Maggie and Sasha's wishes, so that's a start. Realizing Maggie didn't know about Clyde was a bit of a shock. I had assumed because she and Sasha are so close, it would've come up over the years..."

"It wasn't something she ever talked about, except for the once when Maeve took her to the doctor. As for our mother, she went through that long period of depression afterward that most people assumed was because of Clyde's death. Getting it out of her head was the only way she knew to cope. Nowadays, it's different, but she grew up in a time where girls suffered in silence. I think she felt like justice was done...or as much justice as was possible, and the best thing for everyone was to close that door and focus on moving forward. Sasha followed her lead. And Maggie was so young and still struggling from the loss of her own mom. It probably all sort of ran together for her." Kate set her pizza down, appetite gone.

Maybe she should've pressed Sasha to go to therapy when she was a little older. But dredging up something so awful seemed cruel. As silly as it sounded, maybe part of her had hoped Sasha had pushed it out of her head for so long, she'd finally actually forgotten...

Or maybe you just feel guilty you weren't home that day to protect her.

She cleared her throat and went back to the fridge to pour herself a glass of club soda.

"In any case, it's out now and she's finally talking. Let's give it a little time and see if we can get her to go talk to somebody or find a support group."

Lena nodded thoughtfully. "I think that's probably for the best, if she'll consider it. Have you seen Maggie today?"

"Just for a minute when she came down for aspirin and water. She was feeling rough. I heard her praying to the porcelain gods early this morning, so I expect she'll be sticking close to her bedroom. I was planning to check on her and see if she wanted some food around dinnertime."

Lena was polishing off her cold pizza when Kate's phone began to ring. She glanced down and saw Frank's name light up the screen. It rang four times before it went to voicemail.

"What do you plan to do about that?" Lena asked softly.

"I honestly don't know," she said with a sigh. "I've never said any of that out loud before. Heck, I've never even said half of that to myself before. I need to take my time and think it through. We've got a lot of history..."

Lena looked like she was about to argue, but instead inclined her head. "I understand. It's your life, Kate. Just know that you deserve to be happy."

Her phone began to ring again and Lena stood.

"I'll leave you to it."

Kate snatched up the phone as Lena left the room. She considered sending it to voicemail again, but she knew he'd only call back.

"Hi, Frank, what's up?" she asked, trying to keep the irritation out of her voice, and failing.

"I washed the whites with something red and now my undershirts are pink," he said without preamble. "If I bleach them, will it come out?"

She tapped her fingertips restlessly on the granite island. "I'm doing well, and yourself?" she asked, the sarcasm in her tone thick. She wasn't prone to snark, but between her literal hangover and her emotional one, she wasn't in a mood to be trifled with.

"How are you, Kate?" he said, having the grace to at least sound a little sheepish. "I just saw you yesterday, though..."

"Right, and you didn't ask me then, either. But it's been a bit of a garbage few days, for your information."

He cleared his throat and she could hear him shifting in his leather recliner. "I'm...sorry to hear that. What's...uh, what's going on that's so bad?"

"Let's see, my mother is dead, my sisters and I are trapped in a house for three months like something out of a bad reality show, I drank like a sailor on leave last night and I feel like hammered dog doo. Oh, and someone is sending us threats and seems to be intent on blackmailing us. But I imagine since you called and let the phone ring over and over, you had something more important to ask me than about your pink t-shirts, so what else did you need, *Frank?*"

The other end of the line went silent and a tiny, evil part of her wanted to cheer with glee.

When he finally spoke, his voice was low and tentative. "Actually, I can figure it out. I'll just...I'll take care of it. Sorry you're having a bad day, Katie," he murmured.

She let her eyes drift closed and shook her head slowly. "It's okay, Frank. It's not your fault. Look, just throw the t-shirts out and go on Amazon to order yourself another pack, okay? You're due for some new ones anyway."

"Okay, can do," he said, sounding grateful for the direction.

They chatted for the next few minutes about everything from the dog to the kids before she hung up with perfunctory "love you'"s.

She set her phone down with a sigh and wondered if she should've mentioned the potential change of plans with the selling of the house. Probably better until she had something concrete to tell him anyway.

She hadn't been lying when she'd told Lena she had no idea what to do. Listening to her younger sisters talking about their dream business ventures had been electrifying. Maggie and Sasha were taking leaps of faith. Maybe it was time for her to do the same and get out of this rut and this marriage. It would be so easy to get swept up and carried away by the new and shiny glinting just out of reach. Seeing the chemistry between Joe and Lena had only made it more apparent that there was more to life than what she shared with Frank.

But at what price?

She vowed to drag this out for examination once they got on the other side of this. When she was back in her own house, not blinded by some mix of grief and fear and new hope.

One thing was for sure, though, now that this genie was out of the bottle, she wasn't stuffing it back in. She would find a way to be happy, by hook or by crook. Because, like Lena said...

She deserved it.

LENA

"I really appreciate you staying late to see me this evening. I'm sorry to keep you here, but I have something important to discuss with you...about Maeve's estate," Lena said as she took the seat across from Alistair. "And, frankly, it's too sensitive to talk about on the phone."

"Not a problem at all. I'm sorry I couldn't squeeze you in earlier. I'm going away next week so Eunice has been packing my days full until then. What can I do for you, Lena?" Alistair asked, no doubt seeing the anxiety in her face.

"It's Serina McFadden. Clyde's daughter?"

Alistair's mouth went tight.

"Go on."

"Obviously, this is all confidential, as we're trying to keep it as quiet as possible, but since we've been staying at the house, we've been getting some threats. We have reason to believe Serina is behind it all."

If she hadn't thought it before, the fact that the Sheriff or Rusty hadn't come knocking after the whole crowbar incident was pretty telling. They didn't want the police involved, either. It was hard to blackmail someone with the cops sniffing around.

"I'd heard about the rock through the window. I hadn't realized there was more," Alistair said, shaking his head hard enough to make his jowls sway. "People have no respect these days. Your mother, rest her soul, hasn't been dead two weeks and you girls are having to put up with this nonsense. What can I do to help, dear? Name it."

"What I really need is information. I believe Serina's motive is money," Lena said, crossing her legs at the knee as she tried to determine exactly how much to tell him. "She hasn't made a demand yet, but I have the sense that she's building up to that based on the wording of the threats we've been getting. If we don't give in to her demands, I believe she will try to get the police to re-open Clyde's murder case and point the investigation in Maeve's direction. I tried to search online, but couldn't seem to get a definitive answer. Can a deceased person be tried for murder?"

Alistair steepled his fingers in front of his face and hunkered down as he considered the question. "Theoretically, yes. But even there, the motivation would likely be financial. To set a precedent for a civil suit. In the specific case of Serina McFadden, there's also the matter of your inheritance. If memory serves, Clyde had a reasonable life insurance policy that was paid out to Maeve after his death. Clyde's offspring could certainly make a case for being owed those monies, as well, if Maeve was actually the cause of his demise."

Lena's stomach sank. She hadn't even considered that part of it. Her sisters couldn't afford to have the estate tied up in some drawn out case, regardless of the end result. This might be

Sasha's only chance at making a better life for herself, away from all the bad jobs and even worse men that she'd been involved with over the years. For Kate, the money represented an escape hatch from her unhappy marriage, if she decided she needed one. And even Maggie was on the verge of going down a new and potentially very profitable career path that she'd seemed so excited about...not to mention Maeve's legacy.

Lena's mind drifted back to the envelope that Harry had given her and she lifted her head in renewed determination. There had to be a better way. Knowledge was power. She'd lived her whole life by that adage, and she wasn't about to stop now.

"I'm assuming you handled Clyde's will at the time?"

"I did, yes," Alistair said with a nod.

"If possible, it would be very helpful if you could get any records you might have on that, including his life insurance policy, along with anything else you think might be helpful. I need to know what we're dealing with so I can make a decision on how to go forward."

Alistair pursed his lips and studied her over the rim of his glasses. "I don't want to tell you what to do, Lena, but your mother wouldn't want you to put yourselves in danger. No amount of money is worth that. Maybe you should allow the Sheriff to handle this and let the chips fall where they may. Maeve would have set fire to everything she owned before seeing one of you hurt."

Lena bit back a harsh laugh. It wasn't Alistair's fault that the ghosts of Maeve's past were coming to haunt them, but she couldn't deny the old wounds throbbed deep today after hearing Sasha say those words out loud.

Clyde molested me.

She shoved the memory from her mind with sheer, brute force. This was no time for an emotional breakdown. There was work to be done, or the wrongs of the past would only continue to hurt her family.

"I'll keep that in mind, Alistair, thank you. But for now, if you can get me that information, to start."

He sighed, clearly sensing her mind was made up. "Everything from before two thousand will be on paper and in archives. I don't throw anything away, so it's there...it will just take some time to get it all together. Eunice is anxious to head home before her program starts, so we'll start digging tomorrow. This scenario isn't something I've ever run into before, so it will also give me time to look into the laws on other potential financial ramifications if a civil suit is filed. I expect I'll have some news for you in the next few days."

"Thanks. Oh, one more thing," Lena said, almost forgetting to ask the question she had told the others she was coming here to ask. "What are our options if one of us wanted to keep the house? Assuming we're able to nip this Serina thing in the bud, Sasha is hoping to live there and start up a distillery in the barn. If you can maybe come up with some options for us, as far as splitting the equity but giving her some time to get the business up and running, potentially look into permits for her, and the like. Between her goals and Maggie taking the reins at The Luxe, we're in over our heads with regard to how we can make it all work while not necessarily tying up all of Kate's share for a super long time."

"Your mama would be excited to hear all this, I think," Alistair said with a fond smile. "Let's make an appointment when I get back and the five of us can talk about it until we find a solution that works for everyone. And, in the interim, I'll have Eunice pull some info on permits. Sound good?"

Lena nodded and picked up her purse, standing to go. "Excellent." She smiled down at him. "You should know we appreciate all you've done for our family. Maeve valued your friendship, as well as your service."

He nodded his thanks and she made her way out his office door and down the hall.

"See you soon, Eunice," she called, tossing a wave at the older woman.

"Goodbye, Lena dear."

When she stepped outside, the sun was going down, taking some of the edge off the oppressive heat. She paused for a second and sucked in a breath, trying to dislodge the tightness in her chest that had been there since last night.

Drinking and talking with her sisters had been cathartic, but it had also dragged up some feelings that she typically kept buried in the darkest corner of her mind, locked up tight.

Maybe that was what had kept her away for so long. Maybe it wasn't residual anger at her mother, or not wanting the stain of her checkered past to dirty her nice, pristine new life.

Maybe she was just a big, fat chicken.

She let out a sigh and jogged lightly down the steps, making her way across the postage stamp-sized parking lot. She sidled up to her rental car and frowned when she noticed another vehicle well over the yellow line into her space, forcing her to have to suck in to scoot past and slither into the driver's seat.

She shot the beat-up Pinto a glare as she slid her keys into the ignition, but the man seated inside was too busy staring at his phone to notice her irritation.

Jerk.

She pulled out of the parking lot, already thinking ahead to the rest of her evening. She had some friends in the criminal justice department of the university. Maybe she could make some calls and get ahead of this a little more while Alistair got things together on his end.

She flicked on the radio in hopes of quieting the constant chatter in her brain, and had just found a station she liked when she glanced in her rearview mirror. Squinting, she saw what appeared to be the gray Pinto that had parked too close to her sedan in the distance behind her.

Probably a coincidence.

Although, why had it been in the parking lot in the first place? It wasn't there when she'd arrived—she would have never parked so close. And Alistair and Eunice were the only people who worked in that office space...

She gripped the wheel tighter and stretched her tense neck and shoulders. She was making mountains out of molehills. And who could blame her if she was feeling a little paranoid? It had been a trying few days, after all.

As she continued the short drive back to the house, though, she found herself glancing behind her every so often. Each time, the Pinto was still behind her, never getting further than twenty yards out.

On a whim, she passed the turn to Maeve's house and kept going. On the off-chance she was being followed, she wasn't about to lead whoever it was back to her home and risk a confrontation in the driveway.

When the vehicle was still following her four turns later, though, she knew her instincts were right.

She tried to recall what the man in the driver's seat had looked like, but aside from a head of greasy, dark hair, she hadn't seen much. Was he someone working for Serina, hired to keep watch on them, or was this some new, fresh hell courtesy of the La Pierre welcome wagon?

Her adrenaline kicked up a notch as she tried to think of what to do. Like everything that had happened so far, Serina's efforts were designed to make them nervous and instill fear, not cause pain. She likely wasn't in any danger.

And, still, as the car inched closer, her pulse began to pound.

With a muttered prayer under her breath, she lifted her foot slowly off the gas, closing the gap between her bumper and the Pinto even more. The sun had almost set, and despite their proximity now, she couldn't make out his features. She moved into the left lane and the Pinto immediately followed, the driver now making no effort to be discrete. There were only two car lengths separating them as she laid on the gas again.

"Come on, you shithead," she muttered.

He sped up behind her and she nodded in satisfaction as she approached the entrance to a narrow, winding road. With a glance over her shoulder, she jerked the wheel hard to the right at the last second, taking a sharp, illegal turn from the left lane.

She watched as the Pinto sped by, unable to execute the same maneuver in time. With a shaky breath, she laid on the gas.

"Okay. Everything is all right," she murmured softly.

Her rapid heartbeat slowed as the seconds passed without the Pinto coming into view in her mirror. A minute later, she finally relaxed. She was five minutes from home, singing along to an old Bon Jovi song, when the Pinto shot out from another side road to her left.

This time, it didn't take position behind her. It came roaring up beside her like a bat out of hell. For a moment, she almost thought it was going to pass her, when suddenly it came careening toward her, smacking into the door, jarring the sedan sideways and snapping her head hard to the right.

She spun the steering wheel frantically, trying to right the vehicle, when the Pinto came at her again. Running on pure instinct, she jerked the wheel hard to avoid another ramming, sending the sedan skidding off the narrow road, straight into a fence post and smacking her head against the steering wheel.

Her ears rang as she blinked furiously, trying to clear her blurred vision. Panic clawed at her throat as she frantically glanced around, expecting to see the Pinto stopped ahead and a man walking toward her. To her everlasting relief, the car was already speeding off into the distance and she soon lost sight of it in the last of the fading daylight.

For a solid minute, she sat there shaking as she tried to get her head straight. That had escalated quickly. Gone was the sense of security she'd felt knowing this was a shakedown born of opportunity after her mother's death. If Serina McFadden was behind this, she was letting Lena know, in no uncertain terms, just how far she was willing to go to get what she felt was hers.

Lena reached up and turned the mirror down to get a look at the damage. All things considered, it could've been worse. She had a cut on her forehead, and could already see a knot forming, but a quick assessment told her she didn't have any broken bones, so that was something.

She glanced around the car for something to use to staunch the bleeding, and wound up using the sleeve of her blouse. Pushing the door open with shaky hands, she quickly surveyed the damage. Her driver's side quarter panel was badly dented and the fender had seen better days, making her glad she'd bought the extra rental insurance, but it wasn't as bad as she'd expected. More importantly, it didn't look like it would be dangerous to drive. Better to get out of here and off the road as soon as possible. But when she climbed back into the car, emotions hit her like a ton of bricks and her whole body shook like it was on a spin cycle.

She slumped forward and covered her mouth as a choked sob tore its way out.

What had she just been telling herself about not having a breakdown?

But no matter how much she tried, she couldn't stop. She put her head in her hands and cried. For Maeve and for Sasha. For Maggie and for Kate. And for herself, if she was being honest. She stayed like that for a long time, until the tears finally ceased. The sky was dark and the stars were twinkling by the time she pulled back onto the road again.

No matter how scary it had been, she still couldn't afford to report this to the police. Serina's henchman, whoever he was, could've killed her if he'd wanted to. No one had driven down that road since she'd crashed, and it would likely be hours before anyone did again.

No, he didn't want her dead. He just wanted her good and

scared and, in that, he'd succeeded. But until or unless one of them was truly in mortal danger, the risk outweighed the reward. All they needed was someone asking a bunch of questions about that night all those years ago and it could all unravel. The secret Sasha had buried so deep would come to light, people would judge and stare and whisper, even as their mother's name became mud for real this time. Kate and Sasha would lose any chance of making a go of their business idea.

She nodded to herself, more sure than ever. She would tell no one about what had just happened. Not her sisters, not Alistair or Harry, and certainly not Joe.

But that didn't mean she couldn't talk to him...

She slowed to a stop as she approached the old Fletcher place, a wave of relief rushing over her as she saw his squad car in the driveway. He'd mentioned at dinner that he'd bought the place back after he and his wife had gotten divorced a decade or so back. She hadn't even realized where she was headed until she'd pulled down his street a minute before. Once she'd made the turn, though, she didn't turn back.

All she knew was that this was where she needed to be right now. She'd figure out the rest later.

She pulled into his driveway, pulling down the mirror. She didn't want to scare him so she had to make sure she wasn't in too bad of shape. Though the gash on her forehead wasn't that deep and the blood had slowed to a trickle, it had swelled up and was already turning an angry shade of red.

"Something ran into the road and I was nearby," she mumbled at her reflection before stepping out of the car. "No big deal."

She knew how fickle it was to show up after telling him she

didn't think it was a good idea to see him again, but she had to hope he was able to see past that and understand what a confusing time this was for her. Knowing Joe, he wouldn't even think twice about letting her in.

A minute later, she rapped on the door three times and waited. It swung open to reveal a jeans and t-shirt-clad Joe, wiping his hands on a dishtowel.

"Hey, Lena! What's u-," he said, eyes widening as his gaze shot to her forehead. "Geez, are you okay? What happened?" Joe said, pulling her inside and leading her over to a couch in his living room.

The décor was sturdy and masculine, like Joe himself, and the space smelled of leather and lemon furniture polish.

"Um, I was driving over on Hemlock Street and a deer ran out in front of me, so I swerved and hit a fencepost. I was a little disoriented and your place was right down the road. I hope it's okay..."

Guilt pricked at her for the fib, but if the choice was between that and not coming at all, a white lie was a small price to pay for his company right now.

"Of course it's okay. Sit down while I get something to clean that cut."

He walked into the kitchen, which was connected to the living room, and pulled a bottle of antiseptic and cotton balls from the cabinet. "Those things seem to come out of nowhere sometimes. Are you sure you're not seriously hurt? Maybe I should take you to the hospital to get checked out."

"It's fine," she murmured, worrying the hem of her blouse. "It's really not even that bad of a cut. It just shook me up more than anything."

"You could have a concussion and not even know it," he said, sitting next to her on the couch and soaking the cotton ball in the astringent-smelling liquid.

"I might," Lena agreed, wondering if she'd made a mistake after all. "You can take a look at me and run me through concussion protocol if you think it's necessary, but I'm not going to the hospital. Either I'll stay here and you can keep an eye on me for a while, or I can drive myself home."

He opened his mouth to protest but bit his tongue when Lena moved to stand up, looking at the door.

"Understood. I won't mention it again unless you faint or your head falls off or something. This is going to hurt a bit," he said softly as he leaned over her, pressing the cotton to her head.

The sting was instant, but she didn't flinch.

When he finished, she quickly unclenched her fist, realizing with a start that she'd been squeezing his leg.

"Sorry about that," she muttered, cheeks going hot.

"No problem. I'll be back in a minute," he said, handing her the remote, "you can put what you want on the TV."

She settled back into the couch cushions and started to flip through the channels, but she stopped when she heard him talking in the other room. She stood up and crept over into the hallway.

If he was calling an ambulance, she was going to—

"And can I add a side of fries to that, too? Thanks. Sounds good."

She crept back to the couch, flushing with guilt. She really had to stop being so distrustful. Especially since he'd never given her a reason to be. Not now, and not when they were kids.

"I just ordered us some takeout, I got you a bowl of chicken soup. It's what my mama always got for me if I was feeling down. Figured it'd make you feel a bit better," he said, walking into the kitchen and grabbing waters from the fridge, along with a bottle of aspirin.

"Joe," she said, "this means a lot. I really appreciate you looking out for me. I didn't want to go home all shaken up and worry my sisters. They've got enough on their plates."

He nodded wordlessly, clearly uncomfortable with the gratitude, and handed her a bottle of water and two aspirin. "So what are we watching?" he said.

"How about Ace Ventura Pet Detective? It's only been on for a few minutes," she said, flipping back to it in the guide.

"Didn't have you pegged for a Jim Carrey fan," he said, grinning. "But I'm in."

"He's good for a laugh." And if she ever needed one, it was now.

They settled in close to watch the movie in companionable silence. And, when he reached over and laced his fingers with hers a few minutes later?

She didn't pull away.

SASHA

"Want to get out of here for a bit and get our minds off all this crap?" Maggie said, rising as she wiped the dust from her hands. "I'm tired of sorting through all these old pictures, anyways, and my sinuses are killing me."

Sasha rose and followed her toward the attic's ladder. "Thought you'd never ask," she said, yawning.

"I'm just going to fix myself a sandwich and watch some TV, I'm beat," Kate said, standing to follow them as they climbed down the ladder.

"What do you want to do, Sash? We could start shopping for stuff for the distillery, if you want. I know you'd have to order some of the bigger stuff online, but we could hit a hardware store and maybe somewhere to grab some jars and bottles, maybe go to a craft store for label ideas," Maggie said, turning to Sasha as Kate made her way to the kitchen.

"Great, and we can talk marketing ideas, too, if that's all right," Sasha said.

Maggie nodded. "Great. Let's see if Lena wants to get away from her computer for a bit."

"I doubt it," Sasha said, "she's barely left the room the past couple of days."

"Yeah, scary stuff. She's lucky she's just sporting that cut. That deer could've killed her," Maggie said as they walked towards the study.

"We're going to go to a few stores. Want to join us and get some air?" Sasha said, cracking the door, though she kind of hoped she'd say no. Ever since the other night at their impromptu confessional, she'd found the gap between her and her oldest sister even harder to bridge than usual. Lena wasn't being mean to her by any stretch, but she just seemed distant. Like her mind was a million miles away.

Probably in Seattle, where she clearly wanted to be. And who could blame her? It had been one thing after another since she'd gotten here. The deer running her off the road had seemed like the straw that had broken the camel's back.

"No thanks," she said, not looking up. "I have a lot of work to do."

Sasha shrugged and walked to the front door, pulling on her shoes. "Figured she'd say that, guess it's just you and me."

Maggie smiled and followed her out the door. When they got into Sasha's blue Prius, she said, "So about getting your business started and marketing, I have something in mind I wanted to run by you that I think would be mutually beneficial."

"Shoot," Sasha said, turning the car on and starting to back out of the driveway.

"I know I mentioned it before, but the more I think about it, the more I think a partnership would be best for Maeve's brand and both businesses. The Luxe is using well liquor at the moment and it would add a lot of appeal if we could serve something local and high-quality instead. Something that screamed 'Maeve' and Louisiana. And it'd definitely help you get off the ground. I know it takes a few years to age a good whiskey, but we could work with Sweet Maeve's Moonshine in the meantime. I'm looking to get Ruthie from Crawdad's to come over and I was thinking I'd have her create some signature drink recipes using it. We could even advertise for each other if we did it that way."

"Sounds good to me," Sasha said, feeling somewhat relieved. It was risky and a big investment of both time and money to start up a new distillery. She was going to have to use her share of the money from the sale of Mama's jewelry to kick it off, and having a contract with a local business already in place would go a long way towards getting credit extended if she needed it. Failing to start strong in a distillery business without a lot of money behind it could be disastrous. Luckily, they still had much of the equipment for making her moonshine in the barn, offsetting some of the startup costs. It was likely that she'd have to find some kind of day job at some point, just to keep the business afloat until her whiskey was actually sellable, but this would help.

"So what else were you wondering about marketing and stuff?" Maggie asked.

"I love Sweet Maeve's for the peach, but I'm trying to figure out if I should produce any other kinds while I'm waiting for the whiskey."

"What if you started a line of a few different moonshines? The brand can be Sweet Maeve's, and then put the flavor underneath. I can see the bottles now in my head. It's still in fashion to put it in jars, like it's still made in-home, so we could just find a few hundred big mason jars to bottle it up and order some labels," Maggie said, seeming in her element. "I think it'd make sense to go with a rustic vibe and have the labels be that kind that looked like faded paper."

Sasha laughed. "That helps a ton," she said, smiling at her smart little sister. She really was good at this. "How about advertising? How do we get the name out there? I was doing some research online but I still feel like I'm a bit in the dark here."

"Well, what's most important is that you get it into as many local businesses as you can. If the product is high quality, it'll drive sales to individuals, as well as provide a steady source of income because bars would buy in bulk and need a steady stream of product. I'd recommend going into a bunch of places around here in person and giving them a free jar to taste and a business card once you're confident with your product. In terms of advertising to individuals, make sure you get a website and you can buy some billboard space on the highway on the edge of town," Maggie said, her enthusiasm contagious.

"Thanks. I already feel like I have some direction, which helps," Sasha said earnestly, taking a right into the parking lot for the local Target. "I'm sure you'll turn The Luxe around in no time if you're thinking like this."

Maggie chuckled as they pulled into a parking space near the entrance to the building. "Of course. I'm a freaking genius, didn't you know?" she said, lifting her chin with a faux-cocky smile.

Sasha laughed as they hopped out of the car and walked

towards the doors of the store. "Don't make me regret talking you up," she said jokingly. The two of them were laughing way too hard, though probably as much from the break in the constant tension of late as because they were saying anything all that funny.

This was nice. Exactly what she'd needed.

The pair of them wandered around the store, smiling wordlessly, until they got to the aisle where the mason jars were. "These'll do," Sasha said, throwing a few packages of the largest jars they sold into the cart. Though the store, unfortunately, didn't sell in bulk, they'd do to get started and do some testing. She could buy a larger quantity later on the internet.

"Looks good to me," Maggie said, steering the cart towards the registers at the front of the store. "That's it for here, I think. We can hit the hardware store and get whatever else you need to get started."

Sasha followed her up to the register, grabbing two bottles of water at the fridge near the register and putting the jars on the counter. The store wasn't busy enough for them to bother putting in conveyor belts and the cashier, who was one of two working at the moment, seemed almost surprised to have a customer when they got to her register.

"Is that everything for you today, *cher*?" she asked.

"That's all," Sasha said, paying with her card before loading the jars back into her cart and taking a long sip of water as they walked towards the doors. They stepped outside and Maggie slowed, eyes glued to the dented gray Pinto with tinted windows stopped right in the fire lane in front of the store.

"Weird. That's the same car I thought followed me into the parking lot of The Luxe the other day," Maggie whispered.

Sasha frowned then tossed her hair over one shoulder. "At least we're in public. So let's see what they want," she said, striding up to the car. "Mama always said, 'If you can't avoid a confrontation, be sure to be the one doing the confronting'."

She was about to rap the passenger-side window when the driver opened his door and stepped out. He was a little older than Sasha and sported a mop of greasy dark hair, but it was his lifeless, dark eyes that made her wish she'd resisted the impulse to confront him.

In for a penny...

"So who the hell are you? Just a regular run of the mill stalker or another McFadden spawn?" Sasha demanded, walking around the car and putting her face just close enough to his for him to feel uncomfortable.

"Jeb, to you. And I'm the messenger. This is for y'all from Serina," he said, meeting her gaze and smiling as he put a note into Sasha's hand. "You have a nice day now," he said, stepping back into his car before Sasha had a chance to respond. He revved the gas and she stepped aside, heart hammering as he pulled away.

"You're nuts, Sash. Why would you get in his face like that?" Maggie demanded, gaping at Sasha with wide eyes.

"He's basically been stalking us. What was I supposed to do, just smile and go for a handshake? Screw that guy," Sasha said angrily as she unfolded the note.

"I've never seen anyone look more like Mama than you just

now," Maggie murmured, clearly still jittery as Sasha scanned the typed note.

She ignored the compliment and kept reading:

Long time, no see, girls!

Now that I've got your attention, I think it's time we meet up to talk business. Meet me at the gazebo in Tanner Park on Thursday evening. Tell big sis to leave her boyfriend home unless y'all want him to find out exactly what happened that faithful night all them years ago.

PS: Bring your checkbook...

Sasha handed the note to Maggie, mind racing. "First off, it's 'fateful night', you stupid cow," she muttered, trying to process Serina's latest move. It was a bold one—especially having someone approach them at a store in broad daylight—but one they'd all been expecting.

Serina was clearly feeling confident, which was making the hairs on the back of Sasha's neck stand up.

What if Serina and her lackeys really did have some proof? It would ruin everything...

"Let's head home now and tell Lena and Kate, we can go to the hardware store a different day," Maggie said.

"He's lucky I was reading the note when he pulled out of here, or he'd be the one getting tailed for once," Sasha growled, clenching her fists in anger at the implied threat in the note as she walked towards her car. "But you're right, let's go talk to them and figure out how we're going to handle this."

"If we pay her off, when does it end?" Maggie said as they climbed into the car. "And then, it's like admitting guilt, isn't it?"

Sasha nodded grimly. "Which is exactly why I'm going to suggest taking care of it a different way."

Maggie eyed her suspiciously. "Like a crowbar kind of way or...?"

"Not necessarily."

"Don't go off half-cocked, Sash. We've got to think this through and do what's best for everyone here, especially you. If this stuff gets out about Mama--"

Sasha started the car and held up a hand. "We'll talk about it with the others and then decide. For now, I just need to do some deep breathing and meditating."

Per her request, Maggie went quiet. But Sasha wasn't meditating at all. She was thinking about how much she hated being afraid...resented being backed into a corner.

And if it kept up, somebody was going to get bit.

LENA

Tiny rainbows covered the kitchen floor and the hallway as Lena regarded the hundreds of jars sparkling in the afternoon sunlight. She cocked her hands on her hips and shook her head slowly. How many did Sash need just to start?

"A lot more are coming, I'm afraid."

Lena whirled at the voice coming from the doorway.

Sasha smiled an apology and shrugged. "You looked a little exasperated at the jars taking up all the counter space."

"I-- It's alright. I'm looking for a little counter space, is all." Lena gave her a tight smile. "I wanted a cup of chamomile tea."

"To soothe the nerves," Sasha murmured as she stepped into the kitchen and began clearing some space.

Lena nodded. They all needed something to calm them down. They had been around and around the subject a thousand times over the past couple days, and still hadn't come to a solid answer. Alistair had dug into Clyde's will and life insurance policy, but it was taking him longer than expected to get through all the paperwork. He'd promised to call the following morning. Once they knew exactly what they stood to lose, they could finally decide how to proceed.

Until then, everyone was walking on eggshells and would be until their meeting was in the rearview.

"It's a good idea, you know," Sasha told her as she pulled out the tea things.

"What is?"

"The tea." Sasha turned to face her sister. "Mind if I join you?"

"Not at all." Lena shook her head. "I thought I'd offer some to everyone." She gestured to the table and all the jars. "But that might not be feasible."

"Oh, I'll move them. They just needed to be cleaned and counted." Sasha bustled around the room.

"It's a good idea, you know," Lena echoed her sister's earlier sentiment.

"What is?" Sasha's forehead creased in puzzlement.

"The whiskey and moonshine. It's a good investment."

"I--I have to admit, I never thought you'd approve."

"Yeah, it's not like me, is it?" Lena said with a shrug.

But it would put the house to use and kept her sisters busy and happy. What was better than that? And it might even bring some new jobs into La Pierre, eventually, which was always good. Lena liked to think of her family continuing to do some good for the community.

It sure needed it.

At that moment, Lena's phone rang, cutting her thoughts short.

"Hello?" Lena carried her phone out to the porch for a little privacy as she noted Joe's name blinking on the screen.

"Hey, how are you feeling?"

Lena's pulse ticked harder as she tried to act casual. "Much better, thanks. The cut is healing and the bruise looks ugly, but it doesn't hurt much anymore." She paused and cleared her throat. "It's nice to hear from you, I wasn't expecting it."

"I can call back if it's not a good time."

"No, that's not necessary. What can I do for you?"

"I was wondering if you would like to accompany me to the county fair over in Bingham tonight."

"The fair?" Lena repeatedly dumbly.

The humor was evident in Joe's reply. "Yeah, you know, Ferris wheel, cotton candy, rigged games run by unscrupulous carnies. Could be a lot of fun. I'll drive so you don't have to worry about suicidal deer."

"Oh, Joe," Lena started. Surely, she should stay preparing for the meeting tomorrow.

Prepare how, though?

What exactly could she do but fret until the meet up? She was already wearing the wood down with her pacing.

Things were going to hit the fan, that was certain, and who knew if she'd ever see Joe or even talk to him again after that? She sure could use a break from all the pressure and worry here.

A break from the constant fear.

A break from reality.

And there was nothing more steeped in fantasy than a night out with Joe. He'd been so sweet to her when she'd gone to his house a bruised, sniveling mess. And when he'd walked her out four hours later, she'd felt a thousand times better. Safer. More secure, just from having been in his calming, strong presence.

A little more of that would do her a world of good now, when her stomach was in knots.

"I'd love to."

"Great. I'll pick you up in an hour."

"I'll see you then."

Joe hung up without saying goodbye, a habit, Lena guessed, from his job. She put her phone in her pants pocket and leaned against the porch railing.

Another date with Joe Fletcher.

And she couldn't even work up an ounce of regret. For all she knew, her three months in La Pierre could be over after tomorrow. If Serina had some sort of proof in regard to Clyde's murder, there might not even be an estate to split.

When Lena slipped into the passenger seat of Joe's truck a while later, she was already feeling better.

"Hi."

"Hi, yourself," Joe replied.

He sat, one arm draped across the steering wheel, once more in uniform. A uniform that emphasized his broad shoulders, and his natural, rugged build. He watched her intently, his perceptive eyes taking in her every detail.

"Sorry about the uniform, I just got off duty." He gave her a slow smile. "But you're looking gorgeous."

She tried to fight back a blush. Good Lord, she wasn't fifteen anymore. This was ridiculous.

His gaze shifted and he nodded toward the house. "We seem real popular just about now."

Lena didn't bother to glance at all three of her sisters peering out the front window.

Joe laughed. "Should we see if they want to come with?"

Lena raised one eyebrow at him.

"All righty then, let's get out of here."

They pulled into a crowded parking lot far sooner than Lena expected. Joe was just so easy to talk to, she hadn't realized how long they'd been on the road until the flashing lights of the fairway caught her eye.

"So, what's first?" Joe asked as they made their way to the ticket booth. "Pig races, extreme wood carving, petting zoo, tractor pull?"

"Extreme wood carving?" Lena laughed. "What even is that?"

"Extreme wood carving it is," he shot back with a grin.

Lena slapped his shoulder. "Jerk!" she laughed.

His gray eyes twinkled with merriment, and he held out his arm.

She took it like a high-class lady in a ballroom, and together they headed into the fray.

After he bought their tickets, they strolled the fairway. Food booths of every kind offered all manner of fried treats.

"How do you fry milk?" Lena asked, eyeing a sign.

"Freeze it?"

"It would melt."

"Soak the dough in milk?"

"Then it's not fried milk, it's just fried dough..."

"Witchcraft?" Joe suggested.

Corndogs, funnel cakes, and chicken on a stick gave way to less traditional foods such as crawfish boudin sausage and Nutella, marshmallow, bacon, and peanut butter sandwiches.

"If only Elvis were still around," Joe remarked in mournful tones.

Less pleasant scents of dust, animal feces, sweat, and unwashed bodies combined with the smell of food to assail Lena's nose.

"Food first, or on to the extreme wood carving?" Joe asked, one brow raised.

"Educate me."

"They use chainsaws on big logs."

"I'm underwhelmed. Let's eat."

"I didn't realize you were such a connoisseur."

Lena laughed.

"As the lady wishes." Joe swept her over to a candy apple stall with one arm around her waist.

Later, mouths sticky with caramel, they strolled past the craft booths. Lena glanced over hand-knitted blankets, wooden spoons, and earrings made from recycled aluminum. Joe steered her over to a secluded booth and sat her down on a stool.

Lena looked up at him, puzzled.

"Caricatures," he said and plopped down next to her.

Ten minutes and twenty dollars later, Lena held a grotesquely exaggerated picture of the two of them.

Huge eyes with even larger eyelashes protruded below a schoolmarm's bun. Pouty lips shone, so exaggerated she had to laugh. Joe was all angles, and his eyes gleamed, twinkling with an inner light.

When Lena glanced up at him, she found the same look on his rugged face.

She'd never get rid of it, she vowed.

"Next up," Joe announced, "let's grab some tea..."

"Tea? I'm not thirsty." But then she saw the direction of his mischievous gaze. "Oh, no! You don't mean--"

He did.

Despite her protests, Joe somehow got Lena onto the teacup ride. She hauled on the giant wheel in front of them as hard as she could, gleefully taking revenge as she savagely whirled them around in circles.

"Take that!" she cried.

When they finally exited the ride, they were both unsteady on their feet. "Maybe we need to take it easy."

"Wimp." Lena snorted. "Let's do the gravitron next!"

Joe visibly paled as he contemplated the spinning, gravity defying ride.

"Let's do something else first," he compromised. "Ferris wheel?"

She smiled and nodded.

The pair strolled toward the rides, passing the arcade games along the way. Teenaged couples littered the path, crowding around brightly lit stands offering giant stuffed animals and overpriced plastic dolls.

Joe caught Lena's glance.

"You need one of those," he said, tone matter of fact as if nothing in the world had ever been so obvious.

"Joe, I don't--"

"Hush. It's a chance to show off my skills," he drawled.

"Your skills at... throwing stuff, orrr?" she asked, staring around the nearest booths.

"Pitching," he corrected. "Or shooting."

"Three tickets grants you four shots at knocking down the correct bottle. Do that, good Sheriff, and your lovely friend will win the elusive unicorn!" The barker gestured to a fluffy poof with a rainbow tail. "Fail, and, well, I won't give you good odds for getting a raise next year."

Lena laughed politely at the lame joke, but the reminder of Joe's job sent the guilt bubbling up again. The past couple times she'd seen him, he'd asked if all was quiet since the window incident, and she'd flat out lied and said everything was fine. Surely, he'd be furious if he ever found out she withheld information from him about an active case. And rightfully so. But in spite of their history and the pockets of joy spending time with him had given her since she'd arrived back in La Pierre, family was family. If she had to break the law, and his trust to protect them?

She would.

She glanced toward him and couldn't help but smile despite the bubble of guilt in her belly. His fierce look of determination as he raised the dinky gun to the level of his eyes made her pulse skitter. He was really something. And he was trying so hard to show her a good time.

With an effort of pure willpower, Lena pushed thoughts of demented drivers and ugly threats aside again. She was here with Joe and she was going to let go and just have fun.

Lena watched Joe as he fired off shot after shot, knocking down bottle after bottle. He turned to her with a boyishly triumphant smile and she laughed and clapped appreciatively.

The barker let out a low whistle. "I should've known. Here's your unicorn!" He held out a fluffy lump with a plastic horn and crossed eyes.

"My hero," she murmured, taking the unicorn with one hand and Joe's arm with the other.

They sauntered off in search of the most extreme wood carving they could find.

For the next two hours, she didn't think of Serina, or her sisters, or about what to do next. She only thought of how good Joe Fletcher made her feel.

"I had a great time," she admitted softly as they finally headed toward the parking lot by tacit agreement. The balmy night breeze whipped at her hair, mussing her bun. Every so often, their shoulders bumped, knuckles grazing each other's as they walked, and her body pulsed with anticipation.

How long had it been since she'd felt this way?

"Me too." They slowed to a stop as they reached his vehicle and he laid a hand on her door. "It doesn't have to end yet, you know."

His words hung between them, more a question than a statement. And when she met his gaze, it was full of promise.

She should say no.

She didn't want to.

If things went badly with Serina, this could be her last and only chance. One night, no regrets.

"I'd like that."

He lifted a hand and cupped her face. For a golden, perfect moment, the rest of the world fell away. In the next instant, she was wrapped in his strong arms, reveling in his strength, enveloped in his masculine scent. She immersed herself in the moment fully, melting into his kiss, stamping it on her mind like a tattoo that she hoped would last forever.

After all, tomorrow, he might be the enemy.

But at least we have tonight...

KATE

"I don't see how we have any choice."

Kate looked around the table at each of her sisters in turn, stopping at Lena, whose face was impassive.

She was holding up like a champ, per usual, despite the disappointing call from Alistair an hour earlier, but Kate knew she was suffering. When she'd snuck into the house early that morning, she'd looked so young. Her hair loose around her shoulders, a soft smile playing about her full lips, silly unicorn in hand. The second she'd seen Kate sitting at the table with her coffee, reality had come caving in.

The Lena before her now looked pinched and pale, not a hair out of place, as if asserting control over all the things within her power would somehow help her control this.

It wouldn't. One way or another, the ending to this feud was going to be ugly. The only question was, who would get hit in the crossfire, and if the wounds they sustained would be fatal.

"We do have a choice," Sasha insisted. "We can call her bluff."

"I'm with Sasha," Maggie said, shrugging apologetically. "Sorry, but I've seen enough TV to know that blackmailers don't just take their money and walk away. They're like parasites. They won't stop until they drain you dry."

"Or you kill them," Sasha said flatly. Everyone turned their gazes on her and she held up both hands. "What? I mean the parasites, geez. I'm not a murderer, but I'm not on board with feeding them, either. I think we need to take a hard stance. Draw a line in the sand."

"And if that fails? If it pushes them to go to the police?" Kate pressed, still staring at Lena.

"Alistair flat out said that if Maeve is credibly accused by Clyde's family, and the Sheriff's office is compelled to reopen the investigation, there is a good chance we will be on the wrong end of a major civil suit," Lena reminded them. "Worst case, whatever we don't wind up having to hand over to the McFaddens will go to lawyers' fees. Not to mention what it will do to Maeve's name in this town. You can forget about The Luxe or selling liquor with her name on it."

And that wasn't even taking into account what dredging all this up would do to Sasha's emotional state and mental well-being. Kate wondered if she'd considered how painful it would be to have to relive all of that in the La Pierre court of public opinion as everyone tried to find out all the gossip.

"So you think we should just hand them some bags full of money?" Sasha demanded incredulously. "And then we'll just get on with our lives and live happily ever after?" She let out an indelicate snort. "Never gonna happen. Really think about this, guys. If she had actual proof, why go through all of this? Just bring it to the cops and get it the right way. The legal way. I think she's bluffing, and I'll die on that hill if I have to."

"Well, bully for you, but that doesn't mean we all have to die out there with you," Lena shot back.

"What about a compromise," Kate said gently, trying to keep the discussion cordial enough to get to a solution before they came to blows. "We give them an agreed upon amount, and let them know that the gravy train has left the station. That's it. No more. If it works, great. No harm, no foul, and we move on with our lives. If it doesn't, we re-evaluate and go for Sasha and Maggie's idea."

They all seemed to mull that over for a few seconds before Sasha piped up again. "Could be we're doubly screwing ourselves, then. We have to pay them cash and we still run the risk of them reopening the investigation and suing us."

"And I say ten grand or so is a bargain price to pay if there is even a ten percent chance they cash in their chips and go home after they get it. If Serina is as broke as I'm guessing, based on how she looked when Maggie saw her, and Jeb the lackey's appearance, ten grand would be a lot of money to her," Lena said.

Maggie nodded slowly. "Okay. Okay, I can get on board with that. But we've got to agree right now. It's one payment, one time, and no more. I can't imagine what they could possibly have, as far as proof, all these years later that would hold up in court that they haven't mentioned until now."

"That's the problem," Kate said, leaning her chin against her fist. "It doesn't have to hold up in court. It just needs to cause a commotion and get the case reopened to hurt us." She turned her attention to Sasha. "Are you good with this?"

Sasha huffed out a sigh and rolled her eyes. "No. What I'd be good with is dragging this woman out of the house by her hair and giving her a Louisiana beat down for putting us through all this. But I'll go along to get along."

Kate went weak with relief. It might be a short-term fix, but it would at least buy them some time to consider more options and, right now, that was a win.

"I'll go to the bank today and get the money. The estate can pay me back when it's all settled," Lena said, rising to her feet with a tight smile. "Now, what does one wear to pay a blackmailer, I wonder?"

When Lena pulled into the park entrance two hours later, Kate was wishing she'd rethought her outfit, as well. She'd gone with a lightweight blouse and jeans, but she was sweating so hard, it was a wonder she hadn't passed out from dehydration.

"Maybe I should've let Sasha come with me after all," Lena said, shooting Kate a glance. "You're sweating like Maeve at bible study."

"I have nervous armpits, what do you want from me?" Kate demanded. "It's not like I have a whole lot of practice at this, you know. And regardless of how sweaty I am, it's still better than if Sasha gets pissed off and winds up assaulting the woman and compounding our troubles."

When they'd decided how to handle the meeting, they'd also decided it would be better if two of them went and two of them stayed behind as a precaution. If they didn't hear from Kate and Lena in the next fifteen minutes, either by text or by phone with an update, they would make a call to the police. They weren't expecting that kind of trouble, but better safe than sorry.

To her younger sister's credit, she'd handled her position on the B squad with grace, admitting that assault was a distinct possibility if she was within arm's length of Serina.

Lena inclined her head in agreement. "She's a menace when she's angry. Which is why you're here and not her, Sweaty McGillicutty."

Kate glared at Lena and shook her head. "All this time, you're about as funny as a heart attack, and now that we're staring into the gaping maw of danger, you're Don Rickles."

She knew what her sister was trying to do, though. And lo and behold, as they approached the center of the park where the gazebo was located, Kate realized it had sort of worked. She wasn't calm, exactly, but the panicky feeling that had been building since they'd left home had lessened some, at least.

It wasn't like this was life or death. At this point, it was a simple negotiation. They'd either wind up on the winning side or the losing side. It was what happened after this that had the potential to be truly scary.

"There's a car there, but not the Pinto," Lena observed, jerking her chin toward the ancient Corolla idling in the parking lot twenty yards from the gazebo.

Lena pulled in a few spaces down from the car and shifted into park. She glanced over at the other car and visibly blanched.

"What's the matter?" Kate demanded, craning her head to see, as well. The sun was near set, but the overhead lighting in the parking lot meant they could make out the silhouette and general features of the person in the driver's seat—a man who Kate didn't recognize.

"You know him?" she asked, clutching the purse on her lap a little tighter.

She hadn't told Lena, but Sasha had shoved Maeve's old revolver in there before they had left, telling Kate she wouldn't agree to let them go without her if she didn't take it. As much as she hated guns herself, she was glad for the minimal sense of security it gave her now.

"No, I've never met him before," Lena said, turning off the ignition as she turned her attention to the gazebo. "Looks like Serina is already there waiting. He's probably just here for security. Come on."

They both stepped out of the car and slammed the doors behind them. Kate's legs felt like jelly as she fell into step beside Lena through the stubby park grass.

"If it isn't my beloved step-sisters. How have y'all been?" Serina called from the gazebo.

She was seated on one of the benches, dressed in a pair of cut off shorts and a threadbare tank top, a cigarette perched between her fingers.

Kate couldn't say she'd have recognized her in this light, but then she smiled and her blood ran cold.

That smile was all Clyde.

"Serina," Lena drawled, cool as mint julep at a garden party. She walked carefully up the steps and took a seat across from Serina, leaving Kate to follow suit.

"Don't you look just like your mama," Serina marveled, giving

Lena the once over before turning to Kate. "You, not so much. You always were a plain one."

Kate bit back a kneejerk retort as Lena cut in smoothly. "As nice as this has been, we're not here to catch up, Serina. We're here to determine what it is that you want from us."

They'd decided early that evening not to discuss money until the topic was broached. Maeve had always said, "Only fools negotiate with themselves." Better to let Serina lead the conversation and verbalize her demands, in the hopes of getting her talking about what information she had in the process, if any.

Serina took her time answering, pausing to take one last drag of her cigarette before flicking it into the grass. "You know what I want, Lena?" she said, saying the name like it was a taunt. "I want to go back in time thirty-five years or so and make it so that your mama didn't kill my daddy."

She almost spat the words and Kate drew back in surprise. For some reason, she'd convinced herself this was a straight shakedown. Serina sensing an opportunity and taking advantage of it.

Now, though, she had to wonder...

"Clyde was a tree-top father on his best day," Lena shot back. "We saw you for two summers and the rest of the time it was like you didn't exist. Besides, what makes you think Maeve had anything to do with his death?"

"You're here, ain't you? Seems like, if you didn't know it, too, you'd have just ignored me," Serina said, her dark eyes glittering as she leaned forward. "And good daddy or bad daddy, he still used to take care of us. Once he was gone, we lost our house, I had to change schools, my mama had to work three jobs. All while you sat up in that fancy new house y'all bought with the blood money you got from his death. It's a wonder you can sleep at night."

Kate's throat stuck together as she tried to swallow. Surely, these were the ramblings of a druggy and an opportunist. But the longer Serina talked, the less crazy she seemed and, while her nephew had the teeth and skin of a meth head, Serina looked completely normal. Ragged and bone-weary, like she'd lived a hard life, but not like a drug addict. Could what she was saying be true?

"Why now?" Lena demanded. "After all these years? If you thought Maeve had something to do with his death, why didn't your mother pursue it then?"

Serina's gaze flicked away as her toe tapped restlessly against the wood floor of the gazebo.

"Honestly? Partly for fear of Maeve. She had a lot of connections with a lot of bad people back in the day. Mama said it didn't seem worth it to cross her. And partly because, deep down, I think she felt like he probably needed killing." She let the bold statement stand for a moment before continuing. "But she's dead now, too. Passed last year from emphysema. Now it's just me, my half-brother, and his son. All of us, dead broke, while all 'y'all are still living high on the hog. Hell, even that crazy bitch Sasha is doing better than me. Although, maybe if I screwed every guy in town, I could be doing a little better myself..."

A surge of anger shot through Kate and she felt Lena's knee press against hers in warning.

"Be that all as it may, aside from speculation, what proof do you have that Maeve killed Clyde?" Lena asked.

"I'm sure you'd like to know. But that's gonna cost you," Serina said, crossing her legs at the ankles as she kicked back like she didn't have a care in the world.

"How much?"

"That's the question, isn't it? A hundred thousand? Two? How much is enough to repay me and my family for what you took from us? Everything would've been different. Instead of going to a decent school, I wound up going to some dump where half the girls were pregnant at sixteen and the rest were on drugs. The success stories? The ones who got out and," she clawed the air with her fingers in air quotes, "made something of theirselves worked at the bank as tellers. What's the price on that, Kate? Poked around the internet some, and turns out you're a nurse living in the burbs, Maggie has her own company doing something I didn't even know was a job, and Lena is a doctor. Twice, cuz once ain't enough, I guess?" Her laugh was harsh and bitter. "So yeah, maybe Sasha fell through the cracks, but even there...well, she didn't have to be a whore. She chose to."

Lena was on her feet, closing the distance between herself and Serina before Kate could stop her.

She dropped the paper bag on the floor between them and leaned in close, forcing Serina to sit up and crane her neck back.

"Ten thousand dollars," she snarled. "Take it, leave La Pierre, and never come back. Because if you ever threaten me or any of my sisters again, you're gonna wind up just like your daddy. Only this time, nobody will find the body, because it'll be in the bayou for the gators to handle."

Kate stood and reached for her sister's wrist, unsurprised to find she was shaking with barely repressed fury. "Come on, Lena, let's get out of here."

Lena yanked her arm away and swept down the steps of the gazebo with the bearing of a queen. Kate followed, blowing out a pent up breath.

"Ten grand don't even scratch the surface, you uppity bitch," Serina called after them, finally finding her voice and her courage. "This ain't over."

They didn't slow their pace, and they didn't respond. When they climbed into the car a few moments later, Kate turned to find the occupant of the other vehicle stepping out and heading toward the gazebo.

"Well, I don't recall that being in the script," Kate said, buckling her seatbelt. She should probably be irritated that Lena had gone rogue and threatened murder, but there was some sort of savage satisfaction in watching Serina's bravado melt away. At the end of the day, Clyde McFadden had raped their baby sister. His death was nobody's fault but his own, as far as she was concerned. It was a real shame his daughter had a tough time after that.

But life was hard for a lot of people, and they didn't resort to terrorizing people and trying to blackmail them.

Lena thrust the keys into the ignition and paused, pressing two fingers to her temple. "Can we maybe keep that last part between us? I'll never hear the end of it if Sasha finds out."

"Roger that," Kate replied. It wasn't the first secret between them and it wouldn't be the last.

Lena backed the car out of the space and started toward home, clearly emotional and in no mood to talk.

Kate didn't blame her. They'd failed on all fronts, and now, they were right back where they started, only ten grand in the hole. There was no question Serina meant what she said. The wounds there clearly ran deep, and if she did have some evidence compelling enough to get Clyde's case reopened?

This wasn't over, and ten grand would be the least of their worries.

LENA

"This was taken the night of the grand reopening of The Luxe. Your mama was so proud, she was ready to burst!" The soft smile on Harry's face had Lena looking away. She was in no mood to reminisce right now, but they'd already changed their lunch with Harry once, and she didn't feel right doing it again. Sleep had been hard to come by after their disastrous meeting with Serina, and she'd spent most of the morning wracking her brain to figure out what to do next when Kate had reminded her they'd rescheduled for today.

He was lovely, as always, but she was short on both time and patience, and pretending to be interested in old photos was more than she could manage at the moment.

He'd been there since noon and showed no indication of being ready to leave any time soon.

"I'm so sorry, but I just remembered I have to phone into a conference call at work. Will you all excuse me?"

Lena stood and managed a smile in Harry's direction. He looked disappointed but masked it quickly with an understanding smile. "Of course, work comes first, my dear. I didn't get a chance to show you the ones I have of you and your mother on your eighth birthday. She really went all out. Balloons by the hundreds and a towering chocolate cake big enough to feed an army. Anyway, I'll leave them here so you can go through them at your leisure."

She nodded and exited the room, feeling Sasha's disapproving gaze behind her. Too bad. She had enough to worry about without being concerned about whether her sister was annoyed with her right now.

She'd just sat down and logged on to her computer when her cell phone rang. She looked down and saw it was Joe.

Briefly, she considered answering. She'd had a lovely time with him two nights ago at the fair...and afterward, but with every day that passed, it became more and more obvious that it could never really work between them. Not with the way things were. Not just because she lived thousands of miles away. But there were too many lies and secrets between them to ever have something real.

And all of them were hers.

She set the phone down and let it go to voicemail. She was still staring at it when the flag came up thirty seconds later.

Just because she couldn't talk to him didn't mean she couldn't hear his voice...

She pressed the button and held the phone to her ear.

"Hi, Lena. This is Sheriff Fletcher. Give me a call back at your earliest convenience. I need to speak with you. Thanks."

Lena's stomach did a roll and she held her finger over the delete button but didn't press it, instead listening to it a second time.

Sheriff Fletcher...not Joe.

That couldn't be good.

She swallowed hard and pressed the call back button, clearing her throat as she did.

"Fletcher."

His tone was all business and she responded in kind, settling on a polite but stiff, "Hello, Sheriff. Sorry I missed your call. What can I do for you?"

There was a long pause and then a sigh. "Hold on a moment, please." The sound of footsteps and a door closing came through the receiver, and then he was back on the line.

"Lena?"

"Yes?" she asked, her pulse racing now.

"Look, I shouldn't even be talking to you about this beforehand, but I'm going to need you to come into the station so I can ask you a few questions."

The blood drained from her head to her feet and she swayed in her seat, suddenly breathless.

"Lena?"

"Y-yes. Okay, all right. What is this pertaining to, Joe?" Seemed like the type of question a person would ask in this situation, although she already suspected she knew the answer.

"Serina McFadden came to see me this morning. If you can come in now so we can get this over with, that would be good."

Get this over with.

That might be a good thing. Just a few quick questions, perhaps about the rock through their window. Or maybe Tim had finally reported the crowbar incident, and Joe was calling Lena as a courtesy before he picked up Sasha for vandalism?

Or, she really does have a trump card up her sleeve, and he's about to tell you that they're reopening the McFadden murder investigation.

Who knew, but there was only one way to find out.

She nodded and then realized he couldn't see her. "Yes, of course. I'll be there shortly."

He disconnected and she set her phone on the desk with a low gasp.

All right, so she'd pushed Serina too far, and now this was the result. She'd made her bed. She'd have to lie in it. And lie, she would.

She pushed herself to her feet and grabbed her purse and telephone.

As she exited the study, she forced a smile and a wave to her sisters and Harry, who were still gathered around the living room looking at photos.

"I've got to run to the office supply store. We're out of ink," she said with a quick wave.

She was gone before anyone could reply.

The ride to the Sheriff's office was almost surreal. Like she was floating above herself, looking down. When she arrived in one piece, she was almost surprised.

She headed inside and stopped at the front desk, giving the woman there her name.

"I'm here to see--"

"Right this way, Lena," Joe said, striding toward her, a grim smile on his face.

He gestured for her to follow him down a short hall and into a small conference room marked "Interview".

She eyed the two chairs across from one another and tried not to react. If this was a courtesy call with a couple softball questions, surely they'd be in his office, not inside an interrogation room.

"Have a seat."

She did and watched carefully as he sat across from her.

"As I mentioned on the phone, Serina McFadden came in to see me this morning." His tone was even and professional but his eyes were full of something like grief, and any hope that this was a big, fat, nothing-burger drained away, leaving behind cold, bleak fear.

"She brought me this."

He reached under the table and pulled out a paper bag, setting it between them with a *thunk*.

She tried not to flinch, but it wasn't easy. Because she knew exactly what she was looking at.

Ten thousand dollars in cash.

Her ten thousand dollars.

"She also brought me this." He fished a tiny recording device from his pocket and pressed the play button.

A moment later, her own voice poured from the little speaker.

"You're gonna wind up just like your daddy. Only this time, no one will find the body, because it'll be in the bayou for the gators to handle."

The room seemed to dip and sway as Lena struggled to maintain at least a hint of composure.

"Now, I know that's part of a much longer conversation and she's choosing what to share with me. But I'm going to need you to fill in the blanks of the rest of it, Lena, or I can't help you. What the hell is going on here? You told me everything was all right."

She wet her lips, still reeling as she tried to think of what to say and what not to say. "Can I get some water?" she croaked.

His jaw went tight but he nodded and left the room a moment later. The second he was out of view, she slumped forward and sucked in a few steading breaths. It was fine. Nothing had really happened yet. What did he have? A bag of money Serina claimed had come from her, and a one-line recording. The smart play here was to ask for a lawyer.

But this was Joe. Her Joe. The Joe she'd known since she was a kid. Would he really trick her into talking and twist her words to hurt her later?

She didn't think so.

The time for figuring it out was over, though, because he walked back into the room with a bottle of water in hand.

"Here you go."

She accepted it, wincing as their fingers brushed. His lean throat worked as he backed up and retook his seat.

"As I was saying, what--"

"Serina has been terrorizing us for the past two weeks. The note was first, then an email. After that, her friend or brother or someone named Jeb was following Maggie in a gray Pinto. He ran me off the road that night...the night I came to your house."

The words came out in a mumbled rush as she leaned across the table, wishing she could erase the stunned hurt in his eyes.

"Joe, I didn't mean to lie to you, but there are things you don't know...things that it isn't my place to tell you. I'm telling you as much as I can now so that you believe me when I say that Serina McFadden is not the victim here. Now, yes, I did give her that money. But only because she threatened my family. If that's a crime, arrest me. It came from my account and they had nothing to do with it."

Joe squeezed his eyes closed and scrubbed a hand over his chin. "I can't believe this. This whole time, you were being threatened and you kept it from me? Someone ran you off the road, Lena. You could've been killed. And somehow you thought meeting up with these people alone, giving them a bag of money, and threatening them was going to make things better?"

When he said it out loud like that, it sounded extra stupid, and she bit her lip.

"Like I said, there are a lot of things you don't know, Joe."

"Exactly," he shot back, slapping his hand on the table hard enough to make the tape recorder jump. "And that ends right now, Lena. A woman claims you and your sisters went to her nephew's house and smashed his door in to scare her. Then, you tried to bribe her in order to stop her from requesting an investigation into her father's death and, when she refused, you dropped the money at her feet and threatened her life. Tell me why I shouldn't believe her."

Tears stung her eyes and she blinked them back, hard. Like Maeve used to say, crying never helped nobody but Mr. Kleenex.

She straightened her shoulders and stared at him, head on.

"Serina McFadden has been threatening us for two weeks. We have the note from the rock, and the email...and that Jeb guy went right up to my sisters in the parking lot of Target, gave them a note from her, and set up the meeting. Granted, the note isn't signed but he said it was from Serina. He's the one who ran me off the road!"

Joe's jaw worked furiously. "You have two notes. One from Tim, who claims Serina had nothing to do with it, and a second with no signature that could be from anyone. Don't let me forget the email I've never seen or heard about, and a car accident a man Serina knows supposedly caused that you never reported. What am I even supposed to do with that, Lena?"

Great question. She didn't have a reply, so she stayed mum.

"But what's bothering me the most? Is if Maeve didn't kill Clyde, then why the hell did you give this woman ten thousand dollars?"

She hated to do it. Hated that she would have to see the disappointment in his face. The sadness. The disgust.

But she had no choice. Family was family.

"Am I being charged with a crime, Sheriff?" she asked, her tone as icy as her hands.

He drew back sharply, like she kicked him right in the solar plexus. He rebounded like a champ, though, and went into full-on cop mode.

"At this time, we're gathering information on the threat made against Ms. McFadden. Although Louisiana is a single-party consent state and a recording is legal so long as one party is aware it is being made, because it is clearly edited and incomplete, and Ms. McFadden was uninjured, you're not being formally charged at this time. The prior crime perpetrated against your family involving the McFadden family also puts some of her claims in doubt, so more investigating will need to be done. But Lena," he stared at her hard now, his voice dropping low, "this is serious now. Hiding things from me makes it real hard for me to help you here. This went from a note through the window to assault in a car and, now, death threats. This is escalating fast. Let's at least file a report on the accident and we can--"

"If that's all, Sheriff, I'll be going," she said, pushing to her feet. "If you need me to come in again, please contact Alistair first, as he'll be joining me."

She forced her feet into motion and prayed that she could keep it together until she got to the door. She was almost there when his urgent whisper stopped her.

"If there is a real chance Maeve murdered Clyde, I can't just sweep it under the rug, Lena. Fighting for justice is my job. My life's work."

She answered without turning around.

"You can sleep well, then, Sheriff. I promise you, Clyde McFadden got justice, and the world is a much better place without him in it." She turned the door handle and swung it open. "And don't worry, I know the drill. I won't leave town."

She stepped into the hallway, barely resisting the urge to break into a run.

The house of cards had fallen, and she was pretty sure there would be no putting it back together again.

MAGGIE

"Is she ever going to come back down?"

Sasha sat on the couch in the living room, eyeing the spiral staircase as if looking long enough would make Lena appear.

"She's not one for sharing her feelings," Kate said grimly. Her cheeks were chalky with fear, and the usual fine lines around her mouth looked like they'd been etched in with a knife. "And my guess is that she's having a lot of feelings right now. I think we need to just sit tight and give her some space."

"I don't understand why she didn't tell us about the car thing. That's freaking awful. And that crazy redneck should be arrested for attempted murder," Sasha fumed.

Maggie eyed her sister, knowing that all Sasha's bluster was rooted in worry and she got it out by acting pissed off.

A shaken Lena had gotten back more than an hour ago, and had basically swept through the house with barely a wave before rushing headlong upstairs to her bedroom, muttering something about a headache. Kate had gone upstairs after her, only to return ten minutes later looking about as awful as Lena had.

Kate had filled them all in on the basics, including Harry, who was still at the house and currently sitting on the couch beside Maggie, looking completely despondent. He'd offered to leave when Lena came back, sensing there was trouble and not wanting to interfere, but Sasha had asked him to stay. It quickly became apparent that Harry knew about Clyde and what he'd done to Sasha. Maggie tried not to let that hurt her feelings. The more letters and journals they found, the more aware she'd become of exactly how close Harry and Maeve really were through the years. If everyone had a single person in their lives that held them together, Harry was it for Maeve. Surely, that whole time period had been one of the most traumatic of Maeve's life, and if Maggie were to guess, Harry had been the one thing that had kept her from just shriveling up and blowing away.

So he'd stayed at Sasha's request, but he hadn't spoken a word the whole time Kate was talking. As a matter of fact, he hadn't said a word in nearly an hour as they all talked around him, trying to figure out what to do next.

Maggie leaned close to him and patted his hand gently. "You all right? This isn't your problem, Harry. We appreciate the support, but I can drive you home, if you like."

He had taken on a gray, sickly pallor that she wasn't liking much, and the stress was clearly affecting him, but he shook his head.

"No. Thank you, but I'm where I'm meant to be. Maeve would want me to help you girls in whatever way I could." He wet his lips. "Some tea for all of us, maybe?"

Maggie nodded and left the room as Kate dove in to another diatribe about Serina McFadden.

When she came back five minutes later, tea tray in hand, she found the room silent as a graveyard.

"What's going on now? Did something else happen?"

"Alistair called back." Kate had left him a message an hour before, asking him to return the call as soon as he was able.

Maggie waited expectantly.

"Based on what I told him, he believes we have some time—days, probably—but that we should be prepared for a search warrant in the near future."

Maggie absorbed that information, nodding slowly. The ramifications of that weren't lost on her. Even just the one journal entry alone where Maeve had penned her intention to kill Clyde was likely enough to get the case reopened, given that Clyde was found dead not three days later.

Dreams of The Luxe, Sweet Maeve's Moonshine, and all of her non-profit goals came to a screeching halt.

This was bad. Really bad.

She thought back to the letter Maeve had left her. She'd wanted so much to be remembered for something good. Something special. But the part that really had her feeling sick was what this would do to Sasha.

She couldn't meet her sister's gaze as she set down the forgotten tray.

"Well, we still don't know if Serina is bluffing. Seems like if she gave the Sheriff something concrete, he'd have told Lena, or could've gotten a warrant already, right?"

Kate and Harry shared a furtive glance, and a strange sense of dread washed over her.

"There's more, isn't there?" she asked dully. "There's more you're not telling me."

Sasha, who had been gazing out the window as if lost in memories, suddenly stirred. She cocked her head and shot Kate a frown as Kate stayed silent.

"Kate?" she asked, her tone going shrill. "What else?"

"Why do the two of you look like someone just died?" Maggie demanded, shifting a glance between Harry and Kate, dread setting its hooks deep into her heart. "It's bad. I get it. We could lose our whole inheritance and Sasha's trauma could be laid bare. That's a tragedy, but we'll get through. Hell, we'll all move if we have to. I don't care about this town, and I don't care about the money. I care about my sisters."

Harry stood slowly, hitching up his pants as he ambled over toward the office, but Maggie paid him no mind, her gaze locked on Kate as her older sister nodded slowly and let out a shuddering breath.

"That's good, then. Because the only way to make sure we're safe is going to cost us all that, and maybe more."

"What are you talking about, Kate?" Sasha said, her voice cracking with emotion.

"We need to all agree, all three of us. We need to protect Lena."

"Lena?" Sasha shot back incredulously. "She's got money to burn and was willing to walk away from her part of the inheritance from the beginning. She's the one with the least to lose. She'll get a slap on the wrist for lying to the police about the accident and threatening Serina, and honestly, that was on her, anyways. If Mama goes down for Clyde's murder, she has nothing to stay here for. She can just walk out and right back in to her old life."

"That's not true," Kate murmured, but now Sasha was on a roll and there was no stopping her.

"Kate, she's been gone for decades, barely coming around. And when Mama was sick, I was the one—me! —I was the one washing her hair and watching it come out in clumps. I was the one rubbing her back while she threw up her guts after every treatment. And where was Lena? Off on the West Coast, living her best life when I needed her. Just like when we were young. She left us there, Kate. She left me there. Did you ever wonder if she knew? Did you ever wonder if she knew what he was and left to save herself?"

Maggie's throat closed, tears streaming down her face unchecked as she watched her sister pour the remnants of her shattered heart on the floor.

"No, Sasha. No," Kate shook her head furiously, her face full of horror and despair, "you can't think that. She never would've...she gave up everything to protect us."

"Why do you keep defending her?" Sasha sobbed, fisting her fingers into her hair, tears of pent up rage and pain and frustration boiling over.

"This will explain everything, sweet girl," Harry said gently. His own eyes were teary as he handed Sasha an envelope. Sasha took it and tugged out a sheet of paper, along with a second, sealed envelope with a strange seal on it. From Maggie's vantage point, she could see the words scrawled on a post-it note stuck to the second envelope.

In case the police come sniffing around.

"Sit," Harry urged softly. "Read."

MAEVE

Lena,

I'm hoping that, by the time you read this, decades have passed. That I'll have lived a long, happy life, and you and I have mended our fences. That your return to La Pierre upon my death has been easy and free of pain and heartache, unlike your past here in this town.

But if not...if the ghosts of the past come back to haunt this family once I'm gone, and there is any question over what happened that night, find enclosed my witnessed and fully executed confession to the murder of Clyde McFadden. The envelope itself has been sealed and notarized to show that it hasn't been tampered with in any way. It should be enough to put an end to any speculation as to what happened and to forestall any further investigation.

Lena, darling, I know listening to me has never been your strong point, and for good reason. I wasn't always the most sensible woman. But I need you to listen to me now. Please don't hesitate an instant to use this to protect yourself. You came in like a hero and saved the day, but now it's time to put the cape away. The thought of you living even a moment of your life behind bars, because you did what I could not, keeps me awake at night. Your sisters need you, and I need to know you're out there, free in the world to be there for them in the way I never was.

For whatever it's worth, no matter the distance between us, know this:

I loved you most because I loved you first.

Mama

SASHA

"Sash?"

Sasha lifted her head from the pillow and squinted as light filtered into the room from the now open door.

"Can I come in?"

Kate stood in the doorway, her face a mask of despair.

"Yeah."

Her sister padded in, closing the door behind her.

"Has Lena come out of her room yet?" Sasha murmured.

Their older sister's bedroom was down the opposite corridor so there was no reason to whisper, but she couldn't face her right now.

Not yet.

"No. I checked on her a little while ago and she was resting. I'm hoping maybe she took something to help her sleep. How are you holding up?" Kate sat on the edge of her bed and peered down at her.

Last time Sasha had gone to the bathroom for toilet paper after running out of tissues, she'd caught sight of herself in the mirror and knew she looked like she'd been hit by a bus.

And she might as well have been.

"Not great, to be honest, Kate," Sasha admitted, surprised to find her eyes tearing up again. Surely, the well had to be empty by now? "I just can't wrap my head around it all, still."

She'd read Maeve's note to Lena a hundred times by now. It was still clenched and damp in her hand and she couldn't seem to put it down. When she'd first read it, she'd nearly collapsed. It was like the floor disappeared from beneath her, and she was left floating in the atmosphere, adrift.

Maggie had taken it from her unresisting hands and read it for herself. Then there was chatter, lots of whispered words and explanations, most of which she didn't retain. Because at the end of the day, all that mattered was that nothing was the way she thought it was.

"I still don't understand why Mama didn't tell us...or, me, I guess," she said, trying not to sound accusing. There was no question Kate had known the truth for a long time...maybe from the beginning.

"Honey, Maeve came from a time where saying something out loud made it real. If you held your chin up and kept it moving, you could make that your reality."

"Suck it up, buttercup," Sasha murmured through numb lips.

"Exactly. Not to mention, the more people who knew the truth, the more likely it was that Lena would be caught. So it was just the four of us. Maeve, Harry, Lena, and me. And she knew Lena's secret would be safe forever. But she also didn't want you to feel guilty, either. There's so much unnecessary shame on victims of sexual abuse like that. As you got older, she feared you would blame yourself for what Lena did and any of the guilt she suffered because of it. There was already enough tension between the two of you."

A sob worked its way from her chest, coming out ugly and raw. "So, instead, I blamed her for running away and leaving me behind with that monster. That wasn't Mama's call to make. Someone should've told me."

"By the time you were old enough to suspect that Clyde's death wasn't some random act of violence, you had very definitely decided you didn't want to discuss that time in your life. It wasn't for us to force that on you," Kate said, reaching out and stroking the hair away from her face like she was a child. "You'd already suffered so much, Sash. Maybe we made a mistake by not telling you, but we did the best we knew how."

"Tell me again. Tell me how it happened," Sasha said, struggling into a sitting position as she stared at Kate in the dim moonlight streaming through the window. "I tried to listen when you were explaining, but I couldn't think straight, then, and I need to know."

Kate nodded and blew out a sigh. "Okay. Um, so Maeve had gone away on a trip for a few days...a work thing. I don't know why he chose then to start...I don't know why he chose you. I've thought about it a million times, and all I can figure is that Serina had stopped coming to visit that summer, and Lena had been gone more than a year. Plus, Mama had gone away for a night or two in the past, but never for that long. Maybe it was the combination of all those things that made him finally feel safe enough to do it? I don't know," Kate said, shaking her head and clearly fighting tears. "The first two days were normal. He was distant but kind enough. Then he started acting weird. Looking at you in a way that made my stomach hurt. I went to school the next morning, and when I came back, I knew something bad had happened. You wouldn't tell me what, but you peed the bed that night and there was bl--" Kate broke off and pushed out a breath before continuing through tears. "There was blood. I didn't know what to do, and I couldn't get in touch with Maeve on the boat..."

"So you called Lena," Sasha finished softly. "You told her what you thought had happened."

Kate inclined her head. "She told me, whatever I did, not to tell Mama. That she was coming home and she'd fix it. I tried not to, but when Mama got home, she knew something was wrong. She asked me and asked me, and I couldn't break my promise to Lena, but I also couldn't lie convincingly."

"Why didn't she want you to tell Mama?" Sasha asked the question, deep down, though, she already knew the answer.

"Lena knew she'd lose her mind and do something crazy. Impulsive. And then what? She'd wind up in jail with three kids to care for and no one to care for them."

Sasha couldn't even argue with any of that. She'd come by her quick temper and volatile nature honestly, and Maeve would've been more likely to chop off Clyde's privates in a rage and wear them around as a necklace than she would've been to plan his murder in a way that would keep her out of jail.

"Annalise was getting worse every year, and Harry could've taken us, but it would've been a real struggle for him to manage it all. And Harry would've killed Clyde himself...Mama later told me he'd wanted to, but Annalise couldn't survive without him if he got caught."

"So in came Lena..."

Sasha cast her memory back, trying to remember that time in her life, but there was a gaping hole with just snippets that came through in little flashes. Her brain had deleted a lot of those files as a protective measure, which she appreciated most days, but not today.

"Did she stay for a while? I don't remember seeing her after she left until I was twelve or thirteen."

Kate shook her head. "She took a flight in that afternoon and went back the next night. She didn't even stay at the house. She stayed at the Rockaway Motel over in Thorndale. She came back maybe five years later for Christmas one year, and then rarely."

"The thing I don't get...why didn't she just give the letter to Joe right out of the gate? She's had it since Harry gave it to her right after the rock came through the window. Surely, she realized opening this can of worms could be disastrous for her. I don't know how thorough she was covering her tracks back when she was seventeen or eighteen or whatever, but I'm guessing not so great."

"At first, she was hoping it was all a bluff and none of it would come out. That would leave your secret safe, and the estate free of liability. Then, once it became clear it was more serious than that, she didn't want us to lose our inheritance because of something she did. If she handed over the confession stating Maeve killed Clyde, it would give Serina claim to his life insurance money. If Lena takes the rap for it, it has no bearing on the estate or the house, beyond Lena's quarter of the money."

It took a minute for the words to sink in, but when they did, it was like she'd been hit between the eyes with a bat.

"Are you telling me Lena plans to confess?" she hissed, bile rising to burn her throat. She grabbed Kate's arm and gripped it tight. "Is that what you're trying to say?"

Kate looked away and covered her mouth with one hand as she nodded.

"No. No way that can happen. Not under any circumstance." Sasha scooted down the mattress and leapt off the foot of the bed. "We have to give Joe the confession letter."

"I can't do that, Sash."

"Why not?" she demanded, anger warring with confusion. What the hell was the matter with this family?

"Because I swore to Lena I would never do that without her permission. I made a vow, and I won't break it. Not even for you."

Sasha nodded slowly and lifted the crinkled letter in her hand. She stared at it one last time then she tore it into tiny pieces and let it sprinkle to the floor like confetti.

"Good thing I didn't make any vows, then."

She thrust her bare feet into a pair of tennis shoes and headed for the hallway.

"What are you doing?" Kate called after her.

"I'm doing what Lena should've done when this whole thing started."

She jogged down the stairs and snatched her keys off the table along with the sealed envelope that sat beside them. Maggie had been sitting on the couch and looked up.

"Where are you going?"

"To see Sheriff Fletcher and end this nightmare. I won't be long."

And it wasn't. Ninety minutes later, she was walking back into the dark house. The rush of fear and adrenaline had finally abated and she was left like a broken doll that had been glued back together.

Barely.

She closed the door behind her and made her way into the kitchen for a drink. If ever she needed one, it was now. She was about to flick on the light when she stopped short, catching sight of a figure silhouetted in the darkness, seated at the kitchen table.

She hit the light switch and found herself face to face with Lena, her face ravaged with tears.

"What have you done, Sasha?"

Sasha felt something break loose inside her as she looked at her oldest sister, usually so reserved, face ravaged by grief and wet with tears. She rushed toward her, dropped to her knees, and buried her face in her lap.

"I'm so sorry, Lena," she wept as she rocked forward and back. "Please forgive me."

LENA

Lena set one of the glasses of amber liquid down by her little sister's elbow, and took her seat across from her at the kitchen table with the other. Not much had been said since she'd walked in twenty minutes before. Both of them had been far too emotional for much talking. But now the tears had dried and there was a lot that needed saying.

"I know you're mad," Sasha mumbled, her slender shoulders shuddering as she reached for her glass. "But if you were in my shoes, you'd have done the same thing. Don't bother denying it."

She didn't.

Instead, she took a sip from her own glass and tried to think of what she could say to somehow make this better for her baby sister, who already had plenty enough on her mind and heart without having to worry about whether Lena was angry or not.

"I'm not mad. I just would've preferred if you let me handle it."

Sasha let out a snort that was so much like the Sasha of a few days ago, it actually warmed the cold pit in Lena's stomach a little. "You would prefer if we let you handle everything, so no surprise there. But in this case, the result was you going to jail. Sorry, but that's not how things get handled in this family."

There was no point arguing. The deed was done. Sasha had taken Maeve's confession letter to Joe's house, and there was no getting it back.

"What did you tell him when you dropped it off?" Lena asked.

"I just said we'd come across it with some of her affects as we were cleaning the attic this afternoon. I told him that it was in a folder along with a photocopy of it so we didn't have to break the seal, and that, as soon as we saw it, we wanted to do the right thing and turn it in. I gave him a rundown of what was in the envelope, and Mama's reasons why, in case she didn't include that in the letter."

Which meant Joe knew what Sasha had suffered.

Which meant, once the case was reopened, so would everyone else.

"I'm so sorry, honey. That's exactly what I didn't want to happen."

"Don't be. At least, not for that," Sasha amended with a sad smile.

"If we waited, maybe nothing would've come of any of it," Lena said, still struggling to understand. "Maybe Serina would've gone away and no one would have been the wiser about any of it."

"And maybe she wouldn't have. The cops would've started

poking around and you could've wound up in jail for murder. I wasn't about to roll the dice with your life, Lena. Clyde took enough from this family. I wasn't about to let him take you, too."

Lena took another sip of her whiskey, relishing the burn as it slid down her achy throat.

"Is it too hard for you to talk about?" Sasha's voice was almost a whisper.

"I don't rightly know," Lena admitted. "I've never done it, but I can try if you need to hear it."

At Sasha's nod, she continued.

"I got back to La Pierre as fast as I could, but it was different than now. It took me a couple days to arrange for a ticket and all. Kate promised to keep you and Maggie away from him, but I was so afraid I wouldn't get back in time and something might happen again. We didn't have any cell phones or..." She trailed off and tried not to let the dark, sucking memories consume her. "I was frantic by the time I got to the motel that afternoon. I called the house from a payphone and spoke to Kate. She told me she thought Mama knew. That's when I realized I didn't have a lot of time. She told me Clyde had just gone to the racetrack and that Mama an' them were going to the grocery store. I bought a junker for eighty-five dollars from a garage across the street and drove straight into La Pierre. Parked the car over on Melhill Avenue, and cut through the path toward the old house. Kate met me there with Ma' Mere's revolver."

Lena paused and took a long pull from her glass before setting it back on the table.

"I drove to the track and just prayed I hadn't missed him. His car was still in the lot when I got there. Unfortunately, when he walked out three hours later, he wasn't alone. I had to follow them until he dropped his buddy off. After that, it was easy."

So easy, she'd thought for years something was wrong with her. The complete lack of doubt when he'd pulled over to the side of the road—due to her beeping and flashing her lights— and stepped out of the car. The easy lie that slipped from her lips as she approached him.

"Your taillight's out. Don't want you getting into an accident!" The icy calm that settled over her when his eyes widened in confused recognition as she drew closer, momentarily banking the flames of righteous fury that had been dogging her since Kate's call.

Her hand hadn't even shook when she pulled the trigger once. Twice. Three times for luck.

She forced herself back to the present, her white-knuckled grip choking the warm glass as she lifted it to her lips again, draining it.

"Once I knew he was dead for sure, I took his wallet and his watch and I left him there on the side of the road."

She didn't tell Sasha that, as she'd pulled away, she'd said a silent prayer that the turkey buzzards would pluck his eyes out before someone found him.

There were some secrets better left untold.

"And the whole back story about gambling problems and losing that day? Did Mama make that up or was it just the rumor mill?"

"Nope, all true. I just got lucky. Gave someone else a motive. Mama was home with you all by that time of night, so you were her alibi, and that was that. People talked, saying she could've snuck out and done it while you all were sleeping, but mostly everyone was content with the story they'd heard, and Clyde wasn't missed by many."

The silence stretched between them and Lena knew she had to fill it before it grew roots, the way it had for all these years.

"I need you to know that I never, ever would've left y'all there with him if I knew," Lena said, leaning close and capturing her sister's gaze. "I've asked myself every day, from then to now, if there was something...some feeling I had, or some sixth sense that something was wrong with him. If maybe I'm trying to rationalize me leaving in spite of that, just to make myself feel better. But my anger and bitterness toward Maeve is all I remember from that time. It's not an excuse, but it's a reason. And the Maeve you remember is not the Maeve I grew up with. Do you know why I call her that, Sash? Me and Kate?"

Sasha shrugged, tracing the rim of her glass with her fingertip. "I just thought cuz you were being ornery with her and Kate was monkey see, monkey do."

Lena nodded. "That last part is right. But you got the rest wrong. I call her Maeve because she told me to. From the time I was old enough to talk, that's what she told me to call her. She didn't want anyone to think she was old enough to be my mama, so she would pretend to be my sister except, of course, in town, where everyone knew. Having a brat in tow would keep her from hooking another man, she thought. Eventually, once she and your father got together and Kate was born, she tried to switch, but it was too late. She was Maeve to me, and always would be. She was so irritated when Kate started to talk and mimicked me. It was a constant reminder of her failure as a parent. And I gotta be honest, I sort of liked it in a sick way. Every time Kate said it, it was like a little shot. Once you and Maggie came along, I started to realize that my anger was consuming me, but I couldn't seem to master it. Maybe that was my downfall. If I hadn't of been so full of teenage angst, and all in my feelings about how her behavior made me feel, maybe I would've been able to see Clyde for what he was, but it blinded me. That's something I just have to live with."

"It's okay, Le--"

"It's not okay, Sasha," Lena cut in sharply. "And what happened to you was not okay. But don't think for a second that I knew and left you there for him. I could bear anything but that."

Sasha nodded slowly and reached out a hand, and Lena took it. "It's not your fault. I love you, Lena."

She still wasn't sure whether the former was true or not, but she felt better than she'd felt in ages. Lighter, somehow, in spite of all the despair. The next few months weren't going to be pretty. Joe probably hated her, and there was nothing to do about that. Sasha would likely be put through the ringer, and the estate affairs would be in turmoil, but they'd be okay. She'd make sure of it.

"I love you, too, Sash."

Lena squeezed her sister's hand, vowing to figure out where they would all go from here in the morning.

"Can we come in?" a low voice murmured.

Lena swung her head toward the kitchen door to find Maggie and Kate standing there dressed in their pjs. Both looked about as wrecked as she and Sasha, and Lena waved them in with her free hand.

"Come on."

They both rushed forward, looping their arms around Lena and Sasha in a tangled hug.

"It's going to be okay, girls," Lena whispered into Kate's hair.

And for the first time in a long time, she almost believed it.

LENA

The next morning, she did her best to stay busy while she waited for the inevitable. She and Kate managed to finish going through the pictures in the attic. The task was bittersweet now, after having imagined all this and the house itself belonging to Sasha. Now they really were emptying it out to sell, and the thought bothered her more than it should have. This was what she'd come here to do in the beginning, after all.

But something had changed in the past two weeks. There had been a seismic shift and everything looked and felt different. She even found herself mourning her mother at moments as she worked.

They'd all taken a mid-morning break when Sasha made them bacon and egg croissants. The four of them had just set their napkins down when the knock on the door finally came.

None of her sisters moved as she stood.

"Call us in if you need us," Kate murmured.

Lena headed for the front door, her stomach feeling like it was full of pop rocks. She swung it open without asking who it was, because she already knew.

"Hello, Sheriff."

"Lena," he said, his voice low and solemn as he tugged his hat from his head. "Can I speak with you a minute?"

She stepped back and waved him in. Briefly, she considered talking to him in the living room, but then led him toward the study.

He might be here as a courtesy, out of affection for Maeve, to let them know what was about to go down, but this wasn't a casual social call.

She closed the door behind them and they both sat.

"I thought you'd like to know that I spoke to one of the clerks at the Target this morning. She confirmed that Sasha and Maggie were there last week, and approached right outside the window on their way out by a man in a Pinto with a smashed quarter panel. She was actually considering calling us, but he left before she had the chance and they seemed fine when they left. She assumed it was a lover's spat between Sasha and the male driver, since she seemed to be yelling at him."

"Sounds about right, knowing Sasha." Why was he even telling her this? What did it matter now? And why did his eyes have to look so soft and gentle?

"So I went over to Tim Lischio's place to talk to Serina and the Pinto was parked in the driveway, where I got to see the car up close and in person. I noticed the dent had some navy blue paint streaks pushed into the gray. Sort of the same color as your rental car." He shifted in his seat and held her gaze. "When I spoke to Serina about your version of the events that occurred and how much we could figure out by testing paint chips, then went on to tell her about the clerk that saw the Pinto in the driveway at Target where your sisters were harassed, she played dumb. But when I explained that a person involved in planning to run someone off the road could be considered an accessory to attempted murder if the victim decided to file a police report, she realized she may have been hasty coming to the station about the threat you made against her."

"Did she, now?" Lena schooled her features to hide her shock. Was Serina prepared to back off after all?

"Apparently, her boyfriend Jeb has some priors and he would do a good stint of hard time, even if he pleaded to a lesser charge."

She wanted to be happy, and part of her was. At least her focus wouldn't be split between trying to untangle herself from some trumped up charges over an ill-timed threat, and the drama that was about to explode when news of Maeve's confession came out.

"So did you tell her about the letter, then?" Lena asked, unable to stand the grotesque anticipation even a second longer.

Joe's strong throat worked as he stared at her blankly. "What letter?"

Her brain went momentarily offline as she gazed back at him. "The letter that--" She broke off mid-sentence at the sudden intensity in his face.

"When I spoke to Serina, I also asked her if she was sure that you had given her that bag full of cash, or if maybe she was mistaken about that, too. Turns out, she remembered she was mistaken, and was glad I'd gone above and beyond to return it to her. When I left the house, she and Jeb were packing up to head to Missouri."

He couldn't be serious.

"Are you saying--"

"I'm saying that I got to thinking about how sometimes it's best to let sleeping dogs lie, and that maybe you were right. Maybe the world is better without Clyde McFadden in it."

He shot to his feet like the dinner bell had been rung, and towered over her desk, his gray eyes roving over her face as if he was taking in every feature. "I've got to get back to the station, but I thought I'd let you know so y'all could rest easy."

Her breath was stuck in her chest as she struggled to find words. He was halfway to the door and she still hadn't managed it, when he turned back around.

"I almost forgot. Your mama lent me a book before she passed and I never returned it." He reached a hand into his back pocket and pulled out a worn paperback copy of To Kill a Mockingbird. "I don't know what took me so long to get around to reading it," he said as he came back over to set it on the desk. "I'll be seeing you, Lena."

It wasn't until he was out the door that she finally let out her pent up breath in a rush.

She'd lied to him, over and over, and he'd repaid her with an act of kindness she could hardly fathom. Joe Fletcher had done more than turned a blind eye to the truth for her and her family. He'd flat out broken the law and tore the blindfold off Lady Justice in the process.

She reached for the paperback with a trembling hand and picked it up. A still-sealed, notarized envelope, folded in two, slipped from between the pages.

Oh, Joe...

KATE

Ten weeks later...

"Is that what you're wearing?"

Lena's incredulous tone had Kate wheeling around with low-key dread. She looked up to see Sasha sweeping down the stairs in a magenta dress that hugged every curve, with a matching floppy hat.

"You bet your sweet bippy it is. Mama loved magenta and she would think I looked smashing in this outfit."

"Yeah, it's perfect...if we were going to the Kentucky Derby," Lena said, shaking her head ruefully.

A few months ago, the conversation would've had Kate's jaw locked up with tension as she tried to figure out how to diffuse the situation before it got ugly. Now, though, she just chuckled.

"Speaking of outfits, Sister Mary Murphy called and wants hers back..." she cracked, eyeing Lena's staid, gray sheath dress dubiously.

"This is perfectly suitable attire for a memorial service," Lena sniffed, smoothing an imaginary wrinkle from the stiff fabric. She moved smoothly toward the purse that was slung over the back of an armchair and pulled out a black silk scarf covered in a riot of magenta blooms. She wrapped it wordlessly around her neck and sailed past them toward the door. "Ready?"

Sasha's mischievous grin wobbled and she nodded. "Yup. And, seriously, Lene," she added, reverting to the affectionate nickname she used to call Lena when they were kids, "you look great."

Kate agreed. Lena was still Lena. Her clothing conservative, her makeup light and tasteful—a touch of mascara, a sweep of nude gloss, a hint of color on those enviably high cheekbones—but she was also different. Softer looking, somehow. Her hair had grown out to sweep the middle of her back, and she often wore it down now. She'd also stopped coloring it and the result was odd but stunning. A mix of silver and red that made Kate think of mermaids and their mama. Most of all, though, Lena seemed happier.

All these years, she'd been keeping far away from La Pierre as much as she could. At first because of Maeve, but then because it was the scene of the crime...a representation of everything ugly. And now there were no more secrets. Not to anyone who mattered, at any rate.

The truth will set you free...

"Where's Maggie?" Sasha asked, slipping a light shawl over her shoulders.

"Coming!" Maggie called.

She headed down the stairs in a black wrap dress with a swingy skirt that made her look far younger than her forty-plus years.

"Looking good," Sasha said with a whistle.

"Yeah, yeah, yeah, we all look amazing," Kate said, glancing at her watch. "Now, can we get in the car before we miss our own mother's memorial service, please?"

"I told Harry we'd get him at ten thirty, so we've got to go," Maggie agreed.

They all bustled out into the Indian summer sunshine. When they ran into traffic a full mile away from the cemetery an hour later, Lena groaned.

"I told you we should've left earlier."

It was only when they got a little closer that they realized the traffic was all headed to the same place.

"Geez Louise," Maggie breathed, gazing out the window.

"A lot of folks said they'd be coming, but this is surely all of La Pierre and more..." Harry shook his head in awe.

Sasha beamed as she scanned the throngs of people parking on the grass and hoofing it to the location where their mother's ashes would be buried. "Crawdad's holds two hundred, so let's hope they don't all plan to come to the gathering afterward!"

When they pulled into the cemetery, the funeral home director was there managing traffic. He smiled when he saw them and waved them toward an empty parking place reserved for them up front.

The second they stepped out of the car, people swarmed. Kate did her best to give all her attention to those offering sympathy and funny or touching anecdotes about their mother, but she also had one eye peeled, on the lookout for Frank and the kids.

When they'd come so close to losing everything, worst of all, Lena, Kate had gone through a two-week period of what she could only imagine was a delayed reaction to all that had happened, from Sasha's trauma to the weight of the guilt for her part in everything that followed. Bringing Lena the gun that was used in a murder. Allowing their mother to lead by example, burying what happened to Sasha in a deep, dark place to fester instead of dragging it out into the sunshine and letting it heal. She'd wound up having a kind of mental breakdown.

First, had come the relief, which lasted a day or so. Then came something else. A typhoon of pain, so deep, she wondered if she'd ever come back from it. Her sisters had rallied around her, but they were all going through their own transition period, trying to adjust to this new reality. All the drama after the will reading had taken center stage, but when it was all said and done, their mother was dead and she'd taken a piece of each of them with her.

It had been Frank who had come through. Not in a big way—that wasn't his style—but in a dozen little ways. After everything came to a head, she'd planned to do what she'd always done. Shield him from the ugliness and deal with it herself. Only, midway through an innocuous conversation about frozen beef stew, she'd lost it. Everything came pouring out of her. The truth about Clyde and what he'd done to Sasha, what their childhood had been like, her own dissatisfaction that she'd settled for living life on volume five for fear of becoming like Maeve. All of it. To her surprise, when she was done, he was still on the other end of the line and wide awake.

"You mentioned thinking we should go talk to someone...maybe we should, Katie."

No words of comfort. No promises of a better tomorrow. No grand gestures. But it had been enough.

So they'd started going to counseling twice a week, halfway between their house and Maeve's. It was rough, at first. A lot of painful revelations came to light, and she had some real soul searching to do before coming to the conclusion that she'd played a part in their toxic dynamic. She hadn't known how left out he'd felt when the kids had come along. She'd been so obsessed with being a good mother, he'd become part of the furniture, but with a paycheck. Another thing to tend to, but not a partner. Not a lover. And even after the kids were old enough to care for themselves, she'd never come full circle. She made his meals and kept the house clean, but she didn't listen when he talked, or asked about his hopes and fears, or told him she thought he was handsome or funny. She'd taken him for granted as much as he had her, just in a different way, and neither of them had expressed those feelings.

They'd been on a handful of dates since they started therapy, and they'd talked more those nights than they had in the past twenty-plus years. She found that, away from the rut of their lives at home in front of the constantly blaring TV, he was attentive, smart, and even funny sometimes.

Maggie and Sasha had decided to keep the house and live together to save on costs while they got the businesses up and running. It was slow going, with a lot of red tape, paperwork, and planning, but they were both so passionate and driven about the projects that Kate had no doubt they'd succeed. She and Frank had decided together that they would forgo their portion of the house equity for the next two years. She was sure he'd balk, but he'd just shrugged and said that they didn't have the money before, and they'd get by without it, just like they always had. Tomorrow, she'd be headed back home with him to see how things went. She was nervous, but also excited.

She was finishing a conversation with Alistair when she heard someone call her name. She looked over to find Frank and the kids heading her way and she moved toward them, even happier to see their faces than she'd imagined she'd be.

As she looked him over with his old, slightly wrinkled suit and his old, slightly wrinkled face, she realized with a start that she still loved him, in her way.

Would it be enough?

Only time would tell.

She met them halfway, and slipped her arm around her husband's waist and beamed at her kids. "Hey, guys, I've missed you!"

LENA

"She would've loved all this attention," Sasha mused with a bittersweet smile.

Lena surveyed the packed room in awe and nodded. "She really would have. And lucky for us, the Fire Marshall is here, along with half the volunteers from the firehouse, so we should be safe enough."

Crawdad's was bursting at the seams. The burying of Maeve's ashes had been short and sweet, per her request. She was far more interested in having a real ripper of an after-party and, judging by the raucous laugher, music, and drinks flowing, the fine folks of La Pierre had not disappointed.

So far, like so much of the time she'd spent here, it had been cathartic. Like a period at the end of a long sentence. Granted, her time here wasn't up yet. After speaking with the department head at her school, she'd opted to extend her sabbatical for another year in order to create and oversee a series of classes on navigating womanhood, to be taught to at-risk teenage girls in the area. The curriculum, so far, including topics like women's health, identifying lucrative careers, relationships, friendships, motherhood and much more. All of it under the umbrella of Maeve's Way, the newly named non-profit that encompassed all of Maeve's good works. She'd only just begun scratching the surface of all that could be done as she met with female educators and professionals in the area, but the work was satisfying and empowering and she couldn't wait to see where it all led.

"You two better get some catfish before it's all gone."

Lena looked up to see Joe sidling up next to her and Sasha. He was dressed in jeans and a camel-colored sport jacket that made him look like an old time movie star. He held a beer mug in one hand and a glass of wine in the other.

She accepted the lager with a nod of thanks as Sasha let out a gasp of dismay and pushed her way toward the buffet line.

"I've been so busy chatting with everyone, I hadn't even gotten a chance to grab a drink, never mind food," Lena admitted.

She wanted to kick herself for feeling nervous around him. She was a grown woman, for Pete's sake. But things were still tentative between them. For the first month after he'd left the book on the desk, she'd wondered what, exactly, he knew. Despite him calling a week later, she'd avoided him, still unsure if there was a secret between them. After being weighted down by so many for so long, she just didn't have the heart to keep up pretenses anymore, and certainly couldn't imagine building any kind of relationship on top of one. It was only after his third call that she finally decided to answer. And she was glad she did. They met for a drink and, when she'd broached the subject of Clyde, he'd surprised her...

"I just want to make sure I'm the person you think I am. I've done things that many people would view as unforgivable."

"You are exactly who I think you are, Lena," he murmured as he took her hand and laced his fingers with hers. "And everything I'd want you to be."

Since then, they'd gone out a few times, but it had been non-stop action between planning the services for Maeve, getting the classes off the ground, and getting the estate business taken care of. Now that this part was over, she looked forward to getting to know him again. Maybe even starting tonight, after the party was over...

"I think everyone is waiting for a speech," Maggie said as she sidled toward them, her cheeks rosy, likely from the crush of bodies as well as the libations. "You ready?"

When they'd planned the party, Lena had hoped Sasha would do the talking. She was the one who had spent the most time with Maeve in her later years, after all. But the three of them had ganged up and voted Lena in for the job, pointing out that it'd be a shame to waste all those doctorates and not have her write the speech.

She'd done it and had wound up pretty happy with the results. She just hoped everyone else felt the same way.

"Give me five minutes, I just have to do something first." She shot Joe a quick nod and he waved her along and said they'd catch up later.

It took her a full ten minutes to locate Harry and, when she did, she found him outside in the parking lot, hands in his pockets, staring out at the setting sun.

"How are you holding up?" Lena asked softly so as not to startle him.

He turned and smiled, but she could see the tears in his eyes and instantly stepped toward him and slipped her arm around his shoulders.

"No, no, I'm fine. Better than fine, actually. I'm great," he said, leaning in to her embrace. "Your mama would've been tickled by all this action. She would've been even more tickled to know that you not only came, but you stayed. I hope she's looking down on this right now and seeing how far her girls have come."

Lena bit her lip hard as another rush of emotion washed over her. "Your girls, too, Harry," she murmured, tightening her grip like he was a buoy and she was adrift. "Some of us, at least..." He stiffened and she wondered if she'd overstepped. But an instant later, he relaxed and let out a low chuckle.

"Too smart for your own good. That's what your mama always said about you, Lena. But she always said it with pride. I'd wondered if you'd guessed...assumed you had, given all the time you've been spending with me the past couple months. When did you figure it out?"

"I think a part of me always knew. Who else would it have been? But I felt more sure looking through Maeve's journal entries after Ollie's death. She was spending a lot of time with you and Annalise...there was no mention of a man at all, and if she had one, there always was. You know Maeve, in love with being in love. I did the math, and it seemed obvious, then."

"You should know that Annalise was--" he said, stopping short when Lena put a hand up.

"You don't have to explain it or justify it to me. That's the old

Lena, Harry. I won't even pretend to know the type of pain you two were going through at the time. But I recall Annalise's condition when I was a kid, and I know this. There aren't many people who would have stuck in like that. I know you didn't mean to disrespect Ollie's memory, either. I can only imagine how it must've felt to have your best friend die at the same time as your wife lost her identity and mobility. Anyone would need someone to lean on. It makes sense that you leaned on each other."

His double chin wobbled and Lena was worried she'd sent him over the edge, but he gathered himself together and blew out a long breath. "I still have a lot of guilt, but you should know that I don't regret it. Not any of it. Especially not you, Lena."

There were still so many unanswered questions, but she'd filled in the gaps on her own and certainly didn't need to weigh this sweet old man down with any more guilt than he'd carried all these years. Her father wasn't just another nameless and faceless one of Maeve's men who wanted no part of her. It was Harry, a beloved family friend who had been there all along. Who had kept her deepest secret, and supported her and her family when they needed him the most. And now, she would spend what time she could with him before he left this earth, the way she hadn't been able to do with her mother.

It wasn't perfect, but that's the way it was, and she was content enough with that.

"Has Serina contacted you since you sent her the money?"

"No. I don't expect her to. She handled the situation all wrong, but she was right about one thing. Her father was taken from her through no fault of her own and a share of her father's life insurance money was hers by right," Lena said.

It had taken some doing. Both Alistair and her sisters had tried to dissuade her, but now that she knew what Serina had suffered and that she was just another victim of a terrible situation, she wouldn't have slept a solid night if she didn't make good on that debt. They'd done it all through a series of anonymous channels, but they'd gotten it done nonetheless.

Last she'd checked, Serina had purchased a property sixty miles south of La Pierre for a hundred grand at an auction and paid cash. It had cost Lena nearly half her retirement savings, but she'd never felt better about an expenditure in her life. Seemed like a bargain price for peace of mind.

"We should head back inside. I heard tell the catfish was almost gone," she said, slipping her arm through Harry's and leading him toward the door.

When they got back into the bar, Sasha was standing by the jukebox, microphone in hand, clearly searching for someone. Her cornflower gaze locked on Lena and she waved her over furiously.

"Hurry up, people are getting restless."

Lena bit back a smile as her sister handed her the microphone and then linked her arm through Rusty's. Apparently, whatever short fling she'd had with the younger deputy a year or more before had been re-kindled, and if his beaming face was any indication, he was happy as a clam about it. Sasha looked pretty thrilled, too. Who knew if it would stay that way, and, so long as Sasha was happy, Lena didn't care if she stayed single forever. But he seemed like a nice guy, and it was great to see her with someone who clearly cared about her.

Things were bumping along nicely, and Lena looked forward to seeing what the future held for them all.

She took the microphone from Sasha, and held up a hand in surrender as the chants for a speech reached a fever pitch.

"All right, I hear you. Speech! But remember, y'all asked for this," she said with a grin, gripping the mic with now clammy hands. I'm gonna try to do you right, Mama. "We're here today to celebrate the life of the incomparable Maeve Blanchard. As you all know, our mother was a complicated woman. Flawed, like all of us. But since I've spent a lot of years focusing on those flaws, today, I'm going to focus solely on the good parts of Maeve. And on that note, we'll start with her legs...man, those gams were something, weren't they?" she asked with a chuckle.

The crowd hooted their approval and laughed along with her as Sasha let out an ear-piercing whistle that had Lena grinning.

"Her face was the stuff of poetry, her husky voice the stuff of legend. But Maeve was more than a great beauty. She was also a tough as nails survivor who took no prisoners and even less shit. She was a keen businesswoman who knew her place and then ignored it. A lover and a fighter. A fierce protector of her family and the people she called friends. She had a passion for this community, and the people in it. She wasn't big on complaining and pointing out problems, unless she also had solutions." Lena scanned the faces before her, bolstered and uplifted to see everyone nodding along. "Over the years, I've tried so hard to make sure I was nothing like her. It's only these past twelve weeks here in La Pierre, seeing her through the eyes of my sisters and of y'all in the community," she said, gesturing to the crowd, "that I realized what a good woman she was in so many ways."

She held her glass aloft and the room went silent as the crowd hoisted their glasses in return. "To our mama, Maeve Blanchard, may she rest in joy."

"To Maeve!"

Lena swallowed back the rush of tears threatening to choke her. Crying never helped nobody but Mr. Kleenex, after all...

Thanks so much for reading Maeve's Girls! If you'd like to read more women's fiction, come meet the Sullivan sisters of Bluebird Bay in Finding Tomorrow...

Chapter One

Home sweet home.

Celia Burrows stepped through the front door of her house with a sigh.

Part of her was happy to be back in Bluebird Bay, but she couldn't shake the unexpected sense of melancholy that had settled over her on the ride home. She'd had an amazing couple of days recharging at the Lotus Blossom Spa and Wellness Retreat with her friend, Jackie. Her skin felt great, she'd slept like a baby, and she'd had seventy-two hours to focus wholly on herself for the first time in years. But all of that *me* time hadn't recharged her like she'd hoped it would. She was already looking ahead to the yawning stretch of the week to come.

Nate always got on her about that. *"You can never live in the moment,"* he'd say.

Still, she couldn't ignore the niggling feeling that something was missing. Truth be told, the feeling had been there for years, but raising children and tending to Nate had helped drown it out. Caring for her ailing father had done the same.

She'd hoped the spa weekend would help, but if anything, that feeling seemed more insistent. *Louder.*

"Yeah, poor you, Celia," she murmured with a low chuckle under her breath as she set her suitcase in the foyer and hung her lightweight sweater on the bannister. "Stuck in this big, beautiful, dream beach house with your handsome, successful husband. Someone cue the violins."

It only caught her then that the house was extra quiet. Nate's car hadn't been in the driveway when she'd pulled up, but that didn't explain why her cocker spaniel, Tilly, hadn't charged over, tail thumping, the second she'd walked in.

"Tilly, Mommy's home," she called as she turned to scan the marble kitchen island for a note from Nate. She glanced at her watch with a frown. She'd told him what time she'd be home, and he hadn't mentioned going out. "Tilly, come on, sweet girl!" she called, cupping her hand to her mouth and calling up the stairs.

Maybe her sweet pup had missed her so much, she'd decided to hibernate in the master bedroom where Celia's scent was the strongest. That dog hadn't been without her a single day since she'd gotten her from the shelter five years before. Maybe she thought she'd been abandoned again?

Guilt pricked at her as she grabbed her suitcase and jogged lightly up the stairs. But her guilt was quickly replaced with concern as she stepped into the bedroom.

Tilly was nowhere to be found.

Dog and car, both gone. Nate would never put her in his beloved Porsche unless the dog was sick or dying...

So where were they?

She peered around the room again and a strange sensation washed over her...a sense of foreboding so strong, it made her knees go weak. The bed was made, no surprise there, as Nate had always been pretty tidy, but it looked so picture-perfect, it could've graced the cover of *Better Homes and Gardens*.

She walked gingerly toward the king-sized bed, which seemed larger and more ominous with every step she took. Fingers trembling, she lifted the corner of the comforter, and what she found shook her to the core.

Pristine sheets with perfectly executed hospital corners.

Corners so precise, only one person could've done them, and that was Celia herself.

Blood roared in her ears, crowding out the oppressive silence. Nate hadn't slept in their bed all weekend. She'd spoken to him just yesterday morning, and he specifically told her he'd slept in and planned to spend the day working on the boat so not to worry if he didn't answer his phone. No mention of sleeping anywhere but home.

She turned to peer around the room again and something on her vanity table caught her eye. A heather gray envelope propped there, from the gorgeous, custom stationary set she'd bought Nate for Father's Day last year.

Her legs moved as if of their own accord, carrying her toward the fussy little vanity table even though her brain urged her to run in the other direction. She reached for the note gingerly, like it was a bomb, because in the deepest part of her soul, she knew that's exactly what it was.

A bomb that was going to obliterate her whole life.

She glanced down at the masculine scrawl on the front of the silky envelope that simply read, *Celia*. Then she tore it open.

Dear Celia,

It breaks my heart to do this to you this way, but I know how strong inertia is, and how easy it would be to fall back into our normal patterns if I tried to do it in person. I love you and always will, but I'm not in love with you anymore.

The rest of the words blurred before her eyes as the note slipped from her fingertips to the gleaming, oak floor.

How could this be happening? They'd just celebrated thirty years of marriage three months before. He'd even made a toast at the party he'd insisted on throwing. In front of all their friends and family and his business associates, he'd said, *"Thirty down, thirty more to come, and I can't wait. Love you, Celia."*

But I'm not in love with you anymore.

Celia lowered herself to the vanity stool and pressed her face in her hands. This couldn't be happening. Not like this. Not now.

They finally had everything they'd ever wanted. All their hard work and sacrifice had paid off. Nate's business was booming and had become one of the premiere commercial real estate agencies in town. They'd just finished renovating their forever home, a stunning contemporary house with an unparalleled view of the ocean, now equipped with every modern convenience imaginable. The kids were grown and doing great. Max was an accountant in Portland, Maine, two and a half hours south of Bluebird Bay, and happily married to her job, for the moment. Gabe had a great fiancée, and owned a charter fishing boat that allowed him to be on the water seven days a week.

This was supposed to be their time to reconnect. Enjoy the fruits of their labor.

Together.

A sharp rap sounded at the front door and she sucked in a steadying breath.

There were only a handful of people who would stop by on a Sunday morning without calling first. Gabe was likely out on his boat, and Max typically spent the weekends with her friends. It had to be one of her younger sisters. Anna was in town between assignments, so it could be either of them.

Briefly, she considered ignoring it, but her car was in the driveway, and her sisters were nothing if not persistent.

She slipped off her kitten heels, afraid her still-wobbly legs couldn't carry her steadily, and then padded barefoot down the sleek staircase. As she passed the long mirror on the wall, she slowed and swiped at the tears she hadn't even realized were streaking down her cheeks.

No one liked to see a weeping woman—it made people uncomfortable.

The knocking grew more insistent and she quickened her pace. Maybe she was wrong. Maybe one of the kids needed help with some kind of an emergency.

Dear God, the kids.

She had been so preoccupied with her own feelings, she hadn't even considered theirs. What was she going to tell them?

Her heart gave a squeeze as memories pelted her brain like tiny, unerringly accurate bullets.

Nate holding a plump, newborn Gabe in his arms, beaming with pride. The two of them playing catch in the tiny swatch of backyard behind their starter home. Max and her daddy dressed to the nines for her kindergarten Father-Daughter dance.

Celia's chest ached so much, it felt like it might crack in half. This was bad. No doubt about it. But whoever was behind that door didn't deserve to bear the brunt of her grief.

She straightened and threw her shoulders back as she smoothed a hand through her hair.

Answer the door, plead a headache, and get whoever it is out of here as quickly as possible.

She turned the knob, pasting a polite half-smile on her face.

"Thank God! If you didn't answer, I was going to have to eat all four of these by myself, and you know I'd do it. Do you have any idea how hard it is to get a good bagel in this town?" Anna demanded as she pushed past her in a whirlwind of typical, infectious energy.

Celia tried to form a reply as she trailed behind her youngest sister, but her throat was locked up tight, frozen with unshed tears.

Keep it together, Celia, you can do this, she counselled herself silently. *You have to talk to Nate before you tell anyone.*

Spreading the news will only make things awkward once he comes home.

"Tell me about the spa. Was it as glorious as I hear it is?" Anna asked as she set the white paper bag on the kitchen island and made her way toward the refrigerator. "You have cream cheese, yes?"

Celia cleared her throat and nodded. "Y-yes. On the door."

Anna set the tub of cream cheese on the marble island and then paused, butter knife in hand, hazel eyes narrowing. "You look weird. Pale. Did you eat some bad seaweed at that spa or something?"

Celia shook her head and tried to croak out a reassuring *"I'm fine."* But what came out was a wrenching, whole-body sob.

"Celia, oh my God, what's happened?" Anna asked, her face a mask of confused concern. "Is someone hurt?" Her eyes widened as she clutched at Celia's arm in fear. "Dead?"

"No, no," she managed, holding on to her sister like a lifeline. "N-Nate is leaving me."

Where were those dang violins now?

Anna stared at her sister, shocked into total silence.

If she was being honest, her first reaction was relief. Not because she disliked Nate—though she did—but because her mind had instantly shot to several worst-case scenarios. Gabe had gotten into a boating accident, or Max had gotten into a car wreck, or Pop had...

She pushed those thoughts away and tried to think straight, despite the fear-induced dump of adrenaline pumping through her veins.

"Okay. Okay," she mumbled, pulling her sister into a tight hug as she processed this new information.

Nate had always been a thorn in her side. He was nice to her, of course. Cee-cee wouldn't have allowed him to be anything but. Cee-cee and Anna had always been close growing up. Even now, with Anna traveling three hundred plus days a year for her job as a nature photographer, she and her oldest sister talked every week. They saw each other frequently whenever Anna returned to her home base between jobs. Nate had known that bond was unbreakable, so he'd carefully maintained the status quo. Deep down, though, Anna knew he'd never liked her.

Well, bully for him, because the feeling was mutual.

She thought back to Cee-cee, B.N.—before Nate. The girl who used to wake her and Stephanie up in the middle of the night for a giggling skinny dip in the pool. The girl who used to host her own version of *Chopped* on their old camcorder before the show was even invented, laughingly demanding that the three of them make a meal out of canned ham, chickpeas, and peanut butter or something equally vile.

Cee-cee, B.N. had been a firecracker.

Their sister Stephanie had always thought their oldest sister might become an actress or an artist. Something creative, like Anna, because she always saw the beauty in the world.

Nate had been drawn to that wonder and light. At first, Anna had thought it was because he believed it was as beautiful as she did. It hadn't taken her long to realize that Cee-cee was just another beautiful object for him to add to his collection, like his lawn and his car and this house. He liked all of his things pristine, perfectly manicured at all times, and his wife was no exception.

Celia had been no different. She was still a gem under all the polish, but he'd done his best to keep the wildest parts of her under wraps. Anna remembered, though.

Once Nate came along, that all changed. He'd treated her like a princess, no denying that, but he'd made it clear he expected her to act the part. For a beach-loving, small-town girl who preferred a good, sticky barbecue to fine dining, wasn't that the cruelest twist of the knife? He'd done it so skillfully, changing her slowly over the years, that Anna was pretty sure Cee-cee hadn't even realized what was happening. Like a boiling frog, not that Celia, P.N.—post Nate—would appreciate the comparison.

Just watching how he treated her sister was enough to make him a fixture on her "Nope List," but she'd suffered his presence with cool politeness.

Not anymore, though. Now, she could openly hate his guts.

Her sister's trim body trembled in her arms as she wept, and Anna's hand reflexively tightened on the knife resting there. If he was nearby, she would've done a lot more than butter him with it right now, that was for sure.

Speaking of being nearby...

"Where is the bast—where is he, anyway?"

"I don't know," Celia whispered, pulling away as she swiped at her watery brown eyes. "He wasn't here when I got home. He left a note—"

"A note?" Anna demanded, hot rage coursing through her. "He left a *freaking* note? What kind of person..." She trailed off at the sight of her sister's devastated face and tried to hide her anger.

Going off on Nate wasn't going to make Cee-cee feel any better right now. And for all she knew, this was another phase in his ludicrous mid-life crisis, like the Porsche and that stupid goatee. Temporary insanity. If they got back together, anything Anna said now would become a wedge between her and her sister. So not worth it.

"You won't have to deal with him much," Cee-cee said with a sniffle. "You're leaving soon for your next assignment in Bolivia."

Anna swallowed a sigh and shook her head as she took Cee-cee's hand and squeezed. "Not going to happen. I'm going to be here for as long as you need me."

Even as she spoke the words, she felt the invisible shackles closing over her, tightening with every breath. She'd only come back because she'd heard the tension in Celia's voice the last time they'd discussed Pop's declining mental health. It was meant to be a short visit. Long enough to give Celia a much-needed break, but short enough that she wouldn't become like her sister in the process, giving and giving to everyone else, until there was nothing left.

They'd watched their mother do it all their lives, until she was nothing but a dried-up husk of a woman. So insubstantial that even her death from breast cancer had been unremarkable. She'd just faded away, her heart growing weaker until she was gone, like a puffy, white dandelion in the breeze.

It had been so hard on all of them, although it had hit Stephanie, a real Mama's girl, the hardest. Of course, Stephanie had suffered other losses, too.

Anna wondered if Celia had actually processed their mother's death—she'd seemed so intent on healing the rest of them she'd shortchanged her own grief.

Anna cleared her throat and refocused on Celia, who was already shaking her head vehemently.

"Sis, you don't have to do that. It's fine—"

"Shut up, Cee-cee," she snapped, jerking back to glare at her sister. "It's not fine. And it won't be for a while. Just once in your life, can you put your own wants and needs first? Geez Louise, your husband of thirty years just left you, you've got Dad to deal with, and it's going to be a long, ugly summer. Let me help you. Can you do that?"

Celia wet her lips and nodded slowly as she raked a hand through her long, chestnut hair. "Yeah. Okay, I can do that."

"Perfect. First order of business, where is this *note*?" she asked, her tone pure acid.

"Upstairs. I didn't even read the whole thing, to be honest. I was so..."

"I understand. You make us some tea or something. I'm going to go up and get it, and we'll figure out where to go from there, all right?"

Celia nodded again and managed a tiny smile. "Thanks, sis."

"That's what sisters are for."

By the time she got back downstairs with the note in hand, though, her whole body was tense with unchecked fury.

254

"Tea ain't gonna cut it," she said as she stepped back into the kitchen, resisting the urge to shred the note into a million pieces so her sister never had to read what it said.

Dear Celia,

It breaks my heart to do this to you this way, but I know how strong inertia is and how easy it would be to fall back into our normal patterns if I tried to do it in person. I love you and always will, but I'm not in love with you anymore.

I'm sure we've both felt this growing distance between us, so this can't be much of a surprise. For what it's worth, the past thirty years with you has been my honor and I will always think on it fondly. I hope you will too...

Because this town is full of gossips, I wanted to be the one to tell you that, while I've continued to honor my vows to you, I'm ashamed to admit I've been having an emotional affair with Amanda Meadows. We plan to move our relationship forward now that you're aware.

P.S.

Since you weren't home and Amanda has a cocker spaniel of her own, I took Tilly so she wouldn't be lonely. We can talk about sharing custody of the dog once you take some time to process and get into a good, healthy place with our new normal.

Everlasting affection,

Nate

.   .   .

He took.

Her *dog*.

The dog he hadn't even wanted and barely gave the time of day.

Anna barreled around the kitchen, opening cabinets and slamming drawers in search of liquor. No hard stuff, but eventually she found an unopened bottle of champagne chilling in the wine cooler and a jug of orange juice in the fridge.

Morning mimosas. How utterly sophisticated. Nate would approve.

On that note, she pried the cork from the bottle, slugged five gulps straight from the opening and handed it to her sister, who watched in wide-eyed silence from her perch at the kitchen island.

"You're going to want to guzzle about half of that right about now. For medicinal purposes."

She expected Celia to argue, but to her credit, she accepted the bottle wordlessly and did as she was told.

Then, with a silent prayer, Anna laid Nate's letter on the countertop in front of her sister. She couldn't watch. Instead, she paced the kitchen floor and waited.

It didn't take long.

"Amanda Meadows...*our realtor?*" Celia gasped.

The realtor who had sold them the very house they were standing in.

The house that was supposed to be their forever home.

The bitter irony wasn't lost on Anna, but she kept her

expression inscrutable as she studied Celia's devastated, tear-ravaged face, which crumpled before her very eyes.

For the next ten minutes, she just let her cry it out. Ugly, wracking sobs that had her doubled over. Sobs that the Cee-cee of three days ago would've never allowed herself to indulge in. Then, once she had quieted and caught her breath, Anna squatted at her sister's feet and forced her chin up to lock gazes with her.

"I know you're hurting right now. I can't even imagine how difficult this is. But you need to redirect that sadness and get angry. He left you after thirty years and was too much of a chicken to do it to your face. Honey, he TOOK YOUR DOG! What kind of man does that?"

Celia sniffled and, for an instant, Anna caught a glimmer of the old, spitfire Cee-cee, B.N. as she wiped away her tears.

"He did, didn't he?"

"He sure did. Let phase two of sister-helping commence," Anna announced. "We're going to that homewrecker's house and getting your damned dog back."

Get the rest of Finding Tomorrow!

CPSIA information can be obtained
at www.ICGtesting.com
Printed in the USA
LVHW041648040520
654951LV00007B/2193